Oh, she knew his type

Cornball-sexy Santa hat that made him look like a fun guy. A rangy build big enough to make a petite woman feel protected. Gulf of Alaska green eyes with an entire tidal chart of perils. A girl could easily get caught in those currents. Thick dark hair she'd love to rummage her fingers through. Square jaw sporting one of those all-day five-o'clock shadows that—

The small plane hit a nasty sky bump.

"Let's see if I can get us around the worst of this," the pilot said with another of his potent grins. He hummed "Jingle Bells" while banking the plane hard to the left. But upon closer inspection of a towering gray cloud, he shook his head. "Where did that weather come from? I checked twice and this storm wasn't due for a while."

Oh, great. Her first ride in a small plane... and maybe her last. Surely nothing bad would happen—would it?

Not on Christmas Eve...

**Laura Marie Altom's 2002 title, *Blind Luck Bride*
(from Harlequin American Romance),
was nominated for two
Best Series Romance awards
by *Romantic Times* magazine, which called it
"a truly memorable read."**

Dear Reader,

I'll let you in on a little secret…. I want to go to Alaska so badly, I can hardly stand it!

I'm not sure what it is about the place, but it holds a special appeal for me. Trouble is, I don't just want to see tourist Alaska, but the real deal. I'd like to experience winter in Atqasuk and summer in Akhiok. I'd like to earn my pilot's license and land a float plane on a forgotten lake. I'd like to hike the Brooks Range and take ferry rides and pan for gold and fish for king salmon.

The version of Alaska that Colby introduces to Whitney has been somewhat softened. His lakefront cabin always has a nice breeze to keep bugs at bay. In the true Alaska, men have gone down in planes, to die not from injuries sustained in the crash but from insanity caused by whining, biting mosquitoes. Yet the harshness of this vast place is balanced by an unparalleled beauty. To any of you fortunate enough to live in Alaska or to visit—*any* part, I'm not picky—please drop me a note and let me know if it's as fantastic as it is in my dreams.

To fellow armchair travelers, I highly recommend the book *Going to Extremes* by Joe McGinniss. I mentioned the book to the pilot I interviewed, saying that since it had been published in 1980, much must have changed. He laughed and said I'd be surprised by how little had changed. Wow. Since in my neck of the woods, a new fast-food joint or strip mall seems to go up every week, Alaska sounds more intriguing than ever.

I do so hope you enjoy Colby and Whitney's story, as it holds a special place in my heart.

Best (and Merry Christmas!)

Laura Marie Altom

You can reach me through my Web site at www.lauramariealtom.com or write to me at P.O. Box 2074, Tulsa, OK 74101.

SANTA BABY
Laura Marie Altom

HARLEQUIN®

TORONTO • NEW YORK • LONDON
AMSTERDAM • PARIS • SYDNEY • HAMBURG
STOCKHOLM • ATHENS • TOKYO • MILAN • MADRID
PRAGUE • WARSAW • BUDAPEST • AUCKLAND

ISBN 0-373-75047-1

SANTA BABY

Copyright © 2004 by Laura Marie Altom.

This edition published by arrangement with Harlequin Books S.A.

® and TM are trademarks of the publisher. Trademarks indicated with
® are registered in the United States Patent and Trademark Office, the
Canadian Trade Marks Office and in other countries.

www.eHarlequin.com

Printed in U.S.A.

Thanks so much to Alaskan bush pilot Dennis Whitesell.
Your willingness to help a stranger all the way down in
Oklahoma understand the Alaskan pilot's way of life
makes you a hero in the truest sense of the word.

That said, any research blunders are all mine, not his!

Thank you to Mark at Budget Feed in Palmer, Alaska,
for answering my cantaloupe questions.

Thanks also to my talented friend
and fellow Harlequin American Romance author
Karen Crane (aka Karen Toller Whittenburg)
who was so kind as to help with early drafts.

Books by Laura Marie Altom

HARLEQUIN AMERICAN ROMANCE
940—BLIND LUCK BRIDE
976—INHERITED: ONE BABY!
1028—BABIES AND BADGES

Don't miss any of our special offers. Write to us at the
following address for information on our newest releases.

Harlequin Reader Service
U.S.: 3010 Walden Ave., P.O. Box 1325, Buffalo, NY 14269
Canadian: P.O. Box 609, Fort Erie, Ont. L2A 5X3

Chapter One

"You a virgin?"

"Excuse me?" Sociologist Dr. Whitney Foster glanced up from the Alaskan wildlife brochure she was trying to read. But her hands were shaking so badly from a wicked case of preflight jitters that the bouncing words, far from educating her, were making her nauseous. As hard as she'd been trying to learn about grizzly denning—and in the process, forget she was thousands of miles from home on Christmas Eve—she'd been trying that much harder to ignore her too-handsome-for-his-own-good pilot.

As well as being gorgeous, he also appeared to be clairvoyant. How could he tell just by looking at her that she hadn't been intimate with a guy in...well, suffice it to say it'd been a *loooong* time?

"You all right over there? Your cheeks look kind of pale."

Whitney shot the little plane's big pilot her most scholarly glare. "Sure. I'm, ah, great. After way too much school, I'm finally off on the career adventure of a lifetime. What could be better than that?''

His slow grin messed with her stomach even more than the clack of the plane's skis did as they skimmed over bumps on the lake's ice. "Oh, I can think of a few things."

"Which explains your interest in my virginity?"

"Ma'am…" While she clutched the sides of her seat in terror, he pulled back on the yoke, then winked.

What did that mean?

"With all due respect to your bedroom experience or lack thereof, that comment was only my bumbling attempt at making polite conversation. You know, wondering out loud if this is your virgin flight in a small plane? If I ever ask a female passenger that question again, I'll rephrase it."

"Oh. Yes. This is my first time."

Whitney moaned inwardly. Where was a nice dark hole to climb into when you really needed one? Oh well, it wasn't like her pilot would ever get the chance to find out just how accurate his assessment of her had been.

While she wasn't technically a virgin, by the time she found a new Mr. Right, that old Madonna song "Like a Virgin" would definitely apply.

After aiming one more charming grin her way, he returned his attention to flying, thank goodness.

Oh, she knew his type.

Cornball-sexy Santa hat that made him look like a fun guy. A rangy build big enough to make a petite woman feel protected. Gulf-of-Alaska-green eyes with an entire tidal chart of perils. Thick dark hair perfect for running her fingers through. Square jaw sporting one of those all-day five o'clock shadows—just prickly-soft enough to tease a girl into thinking she'd been kissed by a real man, when in reality he was probably a snake.

Like another snake who'd coiled in the bushes, using her to pounce on her supposed best friend.

Ha! As if spoiled Marcie Hawthorne even needed another man—she was an heiress, for heaven's sake! And as for that no-good Rocco Stone—during her last weeks at school, Whitney had heard through the campus grapevine that Rocco wasn't even his name. His *real* name was Ralph Stanley. And he wasn't a senior in premed, but a late-night janitor pretending to be a student at Hillborough College.

After being sweetly courted by him for the better part of six months, after knowing deep in her heart that he was the one, Whitney had caught him sleeping with her roommate, Marcie—his new wife. She'd later found out through still more campus gossip that all along, Rocco had only been using her as an entrée to her rich friend.

Never had Whitney felt so foolish.

She'd thought she was in love with him. During particularly boring sessions of thesis research, she'd even practiced writing *Mrs. Rocco Stone* in flowing script.

Even worse, what with the less-than-stellar example her own parents had set with their love life, Whitney should have known better than to fall for a guy like him—or any guy for that matter.

Her dad, through his many conspicuous absences from the defining moments of her life, had proven that she would've been far happier never even knowing him. At least then she wouldn't have been so heartbroken when he hadn't shown up for her elementary-school Christmas choir concerts or high-school musicals or even her graduation.

Talk about leading by example. If she ever had kids, she'd darn well raise them on her own. She would've been much better off without a dad.

Her children would be, too.

And then there was her mom. Another great example of how *not* to lead your life. Her mom had long since shown Whitney that all males were dangerous with a capital *D*. Trouble was, Candace Foster-too-many-last-names-to-count didn't find men dangerous—she found them fascinating. She didn't just fall for every guy she met—she married him!

As a result, she'd become so reliant on men that she hardly answered the door anymore without asking her latest hubby for his opinion.

Whitney loved her mother dearly, and knew that when her father had left for greener pastures when she was ten, it'd really thrown her mom for a loop. But instead of figuring out how to make her own way in the world, Candace had turned to wedding rings for support.

Whitney, on the other hand—aside from her brief lapse of judgment in dating Rocco—had prided herself on being as self-reliant as they come.

Once the initial rocket launch into a gray winter sky evened into an only mildly bumpy ride, Whitney tried to relax by counting the plastic red berries on the silver garland lining the plane's curved ceiling.

Ceiling? Was that the technical term for the roof of an airplane? Who knew?

When that didn't work, she tried drawing parallels between this trip and the summer sociological field trip she'd taken with several classmates a few years ago. They'd been following up on Polly Wiesner's 1970s study of Hxaro gift exchange among the !Khung San in Botswana and Namibia.

Problem was, even on that remote trek, the bumpiest moments had been when their Land Rover caravan hit a treacherous series of mud holes. Sure, there might have been a few lions watching from the shadows for their chance to swallow her whole, but at least she hadn't had to sit beside them.

Up here, with only the width of her black down coat separating her from the pilot's worn brown leather flight jacket—the one filling the whole cabin with its rich scent—well...

The small craft hit a nasty sky bump.

Whitney instinctively grabbed one supple leather sleeve and the edge of her seat, trying to ignore the tingly-hot waves of awareness that flooded her system from that one simple touch.

"Uh-huh," the pilot said with another of his potent grins. "You're a virgin all right."

As if it had burst into flame, she released his sleeve.

Hmph. Who did he think he was? That hadn't been attraction for him making her fingers tingle, but an internal warning reminding her that just like so many men she'd met, this one was no good.

"Let's see if I can get us around the worst of this," he said, humming "Jingle Bells" while banking the plane hard to the left. But upon closer inspection of a towering gray cloud, he shook his head. "Where did that monster come from? I checked the weather twice, and this storm wasn't due for a while."

"If it's that bad," Whitney asked above the engine's raised pitch, "shouldn't we turn back? I'm okay with spending another night. The lodge I stayed at last night was charming. Crackling fire. Gorgeous Christmas decorations—even better food.

I had steak and a loaded baked potato. I didn't know you had sour cream all the way up here.''

"On good days we have satellite TV and bubble gum, too.'' He reached to the plane's dash for a purple pack of grape Bubble Yum. "So see? We're not all that uncivilized. Want a piece?''

Nodding, she took the packet from him and worked the foil free enough to take one of the four remaining pieces.

The plane hit another nasty bump, but this time, Whitney busied herself with the gum.

"Mind getting me a piece, too?'' he asked after she'd popped her first bubble. "Smells good.''

"Sorry,'' she said over the sudden pinging of ice against the windows. "I should have offered you some when I took mine.''

Unwrapping his piece of gum, she tried not to notice how he'd tightened his grip on the yoke. Now she saw why commercial pilots kept their cockpit doors shut.

When it came to flying, ignorance really was bliss.

Bouncing, pinging.

Bouncing, pinging—then the engine launched into a whirring cough.

"Um, want me to rewrap your gum?'' She'd only touched the paper.

"Wouldn't ordinarily ask this, but would you mind just popping it in my mouth?'' Instead of his customary grin, he gave her a grimace. "With this change in the weather, I should keep my hands on the rudder."

"Absolutely." She nodded. "Sounds like a good plan. Excellent. Best I've heard in—"

"Gum?"

"Oh, right. Sorry." He opened his mouth and she popped it in, and instantly wished she'd kept her thick gloves on to perform the operation. The whispery brush of his lips and hot breath on her fingers caused more distress than the jostling plane. Her stomach flip-flopped, and that odd tingly sensation swept through her again.

Okay, what was going on?

No case of airsickness she'd ever heard of started with a gnawing, all-consuming—completely irrational—urge to touch one's pilot!

"Thanks for the gum," he said.

"You're welcome." *And thank you for being so darned hot that at least looking at you is taking my mind off this lousy weather.*

TEN MINUTES LATER, the icy assault had let up, and Colby Davis wondered if he should use the time to try calming his passenger. The flight and weather were routine to him, but judging by her wide-eyed stare, she wasn't likely to be a repeat customer.

"You know," he said, "back at the lake, I was in such a hurry to load your gear I didn't get a chance to properly introduce myself.'' Left hand on the stick, he offered her his right. ''I'm Colby.''

''Whitney,'' she said. ''Nice to meet you.''

His grip swallowed her slim fingers, triggering not only instant awareness and heat, but that infernal protective streak that had gotten him into more trouble than he cared to remember.

She's just a paying customer, he told himself as he released her hand.

Even so, he cranked up the heater to warm her icy fingertips.

Since she didn't seem all that talkative at the moment, he took a turn at tossing the conversational ball. ''You said you're a sociologist. What're you doing with those yahoos up at the oil site?''

''The company I work for back in Chicago performs employee evaluations for other companies. In this case, Global Oil. They have a high turnover rate at remote sites like this and want me to study how isolation affects the crew, then develop ways to counteract it.''

Colby nodded.

Sounded like a load of bull to him, but he wasn't about to tell her that. Alaska either made a man or broke him. If the state were equated to a woman, she wouldn't be kind or forgiving, but she was fair. As long as a man kept his wits about him, he'd be okay.

Colby happened to love Alaska.

His friend Tanner, on the other hand, was giving serious thought to chucking it all in. His plan was to somehow sell his failing fishing lodge and then head to the lower forty-eight to seek his fortune. At the first sign of trouble, his wife Jenny had bailed. Tanner probably thought he could chase her down and work things out, but Colby had seen this sort of thing happen more times than he could remember.

You either loved Alaska or hated it, and you sure as hell couldn't force a woman to love it any more than you could force her to love a man.

Colby clenched his jaw.

Damn shame about those two. They'd been good together.

"How much longer?" Whitney asked, tracing a pattern in the frost on the inside of her window.

"'Bout thirty minutes. Maybe longer with this head wind."

She nodded, and blew a bubble at the same time he did. They both laughed.

"Feeling better?" he asked.

"Yeah," she said with her first genuine smile of the day. "Never underestimate the calming powers of a good grape bubble."

Grape bubbles, hell. What he'd underestimated was the power of her grin, which was warming him way more than the plane's heater.

Colby had time for one last chuckle before all hell broke loose.

Ice pellets spattered the windshield like bullets, one of them cracking the glass. Ferocious winds buffeted the tiny plane like a moose swinging its rack at a gnat.

"Hold on!" Colby said as the plane lost altitude, dipping into a terrifying valley only to rise back up to a treacherous, turbulence-filled peak.

He risked a sideways glance and saw his passenger's teeth chattering. From fear? Or was it just the icy fingers of wind slicing through every air hole in the plane? The heater wasn't coming close to keeping up.

The ice pellets had turned to freezing rain, coating the windshield.

Whitney watched her pilot press a button that made some sort of de-icing liquid squirt from the windshield wipers. It helped a bit, but hardly solved the icy problem.

The engine struggled to outpace the wind, whining from the effort.

"You ever been in this tight a jam before?" she managed to ask past her dry throat.

"This?" His white-toothed smile held enough raw sex appeal to set her senses on edge again. The plane's every bounce jingled the bell on his Santa hat, distracting her even more. "This is nothing. You should've been here the time I—"

The engine coughed and sputtered, then died.

"Okay," he said, fiddling with knobs and controls. "Now, we might be in a speck of trouble. But just a speck." He held his thumb and forefinger barely apart, but that didn't do much to calm her nerves.

"Oh God," she said. Inside, she said a little more. She wasn't ready to die.

She wasn't anywhere near ready to die.

She'd really looked forward to getting out of school. Acing her first field assignment—a two-month gig. Renewing her relationship with her mom. While Whitney never planned to marry—her mother had done enough of that for the both of them—she did very much want to have kids one day. And as for what would *make* those kids—the sex—she wanted the chance to try it again.

"Oh, God," she wailed. "I don't wanna die. I *really* don't wanna die."

"Me neither, sweetie." He held the yoke so tight that his face reddened and a vein popped on his forehead.

"Mayday, mayday," he called into the radio, relaying their location.

No one answered.

"Think anyone heard you?" Whitney asked above the racket from the storm.

"Hard to say." He gave the dash a good hard thwack, then fiddled with more knobs.

And then a rogue gust caught them, aiding in their not-so-gentle glide to the ground.

"You filed a flight plan, right?"

"Uh-huh."

"So then just as soon as we land, someone'll be out to get us?"

"That'd be nice."

"But…"

"But, too bad for us, if I know this area as well as I think I do, we're coming down smack dab in the middle of some of the roughest terrain on God's white earth."

He radioed for help again.

Twisted still more controls.

Something scraped the bottom of the plane. Tree-tops? Rock?

The plane lurched, then continued its rapid descent.

Jaw hard and knuckles white from fighting the forces trying to rip the yoke from his hand, Colby said, "You the praying kind?"

"Not particularly."

"Now might be a good time to start."

Chapter Two

"Whitney?" Minutes after ditching the plane in a powdery-soft snow bowl angels must have guided him to find, Colby gave his fare a light shake.

He felt his way in the darkness to an equipment box he kept beneath his seat, reaching inside for a flashlight. He flicked it on, shining it her way.

No blood. Good. *Very* good.

Her complexion was waxy, but considering what they'd just been through, that was no biggie.

Garland had fallen on her right shoulder. He flicked it off of her.

Leaning back in his seat, he slammed the yoke with the heel of his hand. Dammit, how had he let this happen?

He knew the route.

Knew the weather.

His landing had been safe but sloppy. The left wing had been sheared, throwing the whole ride off balance, plowing them deep into the snow.

By his calculations, this storm should've taken at least another day to barrel through this part of the state. He should've had more than enough time to safely deliver his fare to the drilling site, then get himself back to a crackling fire, a bowl of Nugget's steaming beef stew and that special Christmas Eve Lakers game on ESPN.

His fare.

Gazing at her now, he frowned.

From the second she'd stepped off the snow-crusted dock and into his plane, Whitney had become his responsibility.

And now?

He raked his fingers through his hair.

Now, he could quite possibly be responsible for her death. He wished he had a keg of the best beer in the world—Moose's Tooth Fairweather IPA—to counteract that sobering thought.

"Hello? Whitney?" he asked, giving her another shake. He held his open palm just below her nose. Puffs of breath warmed his hand. Whew. She was very much alive. Breathing normally—or as close to it as could be expected.

Colby ran the light over her legs, finding them surprisingly long for her small frame. And straight—thank God. Her arms looked good, too. The last thing he needed was broken limbs. He would have enough trouble just figuring out how to keep her warm.

Well…one tried and true method of keeping warm sprang to mind, but while snuggling naked would certainly do the trick, it hardly seemed professional. "Whitney? Can you hear me?"

Her eyelashes fluttered.

He shone the light in her eyes and she winced.

"Sorry," he said, relieved to see her awake. "You all right?"

"Is this going to make me late for work?"

Grinning, he pulled her into a hug. "Ahh, one thing's for sure, your sass is still alive and well. You're gonna be just fine."

"Am I? I mean, are we?"

"Honestly?" He released her and glanced out the window at the white wall of snow curtaining the plane. Turning away from that unpleasant sight, he said, "I don't know. I've been in more desperate jams."

"But?"

"This one's looking worse by the minute. That's not to say we don't have a great chance of rescue. Our ELT transmitter's on. Course, the signal's operated by radio, so the odds of it getting out in this weather are slim, but I did radio our coordinates out on the emergency channel. And if we make it through the storm and the weather clears, I can fire the signal pistol if we see any search planes…."

"But?"

"Quit with the buts, okay?"

"Sorry. I'm a bottom-line kind of girl. Give me the worst-case scenario. We're going to be squeezed in here together for what? Maybe one or two days?"

His lips settled in a grim line.

"More like a week? I packed tons of snack food, you know, since I didn't know what provisions they'd have at the site. I've got Twinkies and three kinds of Little Debbie cupcakes and graham crackers and granola bars. And Snickers—lots and lots of Snickers. We should be fine for food. And jeez, with all that snow, we won't even have to worry about water."

She shivered. "Any chance of you fixing the heater? It's freezing in here." She tried making a smoke ring from her visible breath but failed. "What? Why are you quiet all of a sudden?"

He swallowed hard.

For a manly guy like him, she wasn't sure if that was a good sign or bad. "Does that look of yours mean the heater can't be fixed?"

He nodded.

"Okay, but we've got food and water. That's good, right?"

"I'm sorry."

"No, no, don't be sorry. Sorry is bad. Just a minute ago, when I said I was a bottom-line girl? Well, I lied. I'm really more the ostrich type. That's why I prefer flying commercial. Because that way flying is like a Disney ride. You know, magic. I just pop my window shade down, slip on my headphones and before you know it—poof—we're magically there.'' Even the tears streaming down her cheeks felt cold. She swiped them away to keep them from freezing.

Colby unfastened his seat belt and angled himself to face her. For a long time he just stared at her, and then he skimmed the warm backs of his fingers against her cheek. ''Whitney, I'm sorry. *Really* sorry, but the plain truth is that in these conditions, well…it's gonna be pretty dangerous for rescue crews to go out. If we make it till morning, and the storm clears, well, that could be a whole new ball game. I've got snowshoes and a hatchet. I could turn all Paul Bunyan and cut down a whole damn forest to keep us warm. Problem is, by midnight tonight, this high up, we could be facing temps of fifty below.''

''But you don't know that for sure, right?''

He dropped his stare.

''Oh, God, this *is* bad. I've got so many plans for the future.'' She looked to her lap, then at him. ''I'm sure you've got plenty, too. I'd hoped to spend next Christmas with my mom—just couldn't bring myself to do it this year. And my job…it was just getting good. I've always dreamed of becoming famous in my field.''

''I didn't know there were any famous sociologists—but, hey, what do I know? If they give out Nobel prizes for that kind of thing, I'm sure you're a shoo-in.''

His big grin started up that tingling again, and his words made her retract every comparison she'd earlier made between him and Rocco. This man was nothing like Rocco.

Colby was considerate and sweet and funny—just the sort of man only thirty minutes earlier she would never have believed even existed.

She licked her lips, realizing anew how close they were sitting to each other. Colby's face was only inches from hers—close enough that even in the dim glow of the flashlight resting on his lap, she could see the tenderness in his gaze. Even better was the way heat from his breath caressed her lips, teasing them into a smile as the grapey-sweet smell of his gum tickled her nose.

''If I didn't have this gum in my mouth,'' he said, ''I'd kiss you.''

''If you can reach behind my seat for my purse, I have some tissue.''

''Oh, you do, do you?''

Was that a twinkle lighting his eyes?

Her heart skipped a beat.

Here she was quite possibly on the verge of dying. How could fate be so cruel as to finally introduce her to the last living nice guy only to—maybe—snatch him away mere hours later?

He found her purse, and she dug through for tissues to dispose of their gum. For an instant, as she rummaged through everyday items like lip gloss and aspirin and the little sewing kit she never left home without, life felt normal. But then she glanced at the frosty window and the odd angle of their seats and knew Colby could very well be right.

This might be the end for them both.

At this very moment, they could be down to only hours to live.

Her breath caught in her throat.

Hours? That was it?

How was that possible?

She swallowed hard.

"Hey." Her pilot leaned even closer to brush away her tears. "What's with the waterworks?"

Looking away, she shrugged.

"You're not upset over my gloom-and-doom routine, are you? Because if anyone can rescue us, it's the guys in Kodiak Gorge. They're top-notch."

"Really?"

"Yeah. Oh, hell, yeah." He hugged her again. Never had she felt safer and more secure than in this virtual stranger's arms. His touch warmed not just her body, but her soul.

When she'd recovered from her latest bout of tears, she pulled back just far enough to look at him. "Thank you," she said. "I needed a hug."

"Ho, ho, ho…" He jingled the bell on his Santa hat. "I'm all about making the little—and big—girls happy."

She giggled, and then he was inching closer, closer, until the heat of his hands on her arms had nothing on the glorious blaze of his lips. His kiss started out soft, maybe even a little teasing with those sugary grapes still flavoring his breath. Then he increased the pressure and she found herself not just going along for the ride, as she had with the few other men in her life, but meeting his tongue thrust for spellbinding thrust.

Never had she experienced such a myriad of reactions all at once, from fascination and ecstasy to brazen curiosity. If just kissing Colby felt this good…

He drew back. "Wow. Sorry. That wasn't very professional."

Shaking her head, she touched her fingers to his still-moist lips. "It might not've been professional, but it was very nice."

Cupping her face in his big hands, he murmured, "Just nice?"

"I said *very*."

"Oh, well, in that case…may I kiss you again?"

Teary-eyed, she nodded.

And he did kiss her. Again and again.

Whitney groaned, repositioning herself to sink more deeply into his welcome embrace.

An hour earlier, she hadn't thought feelings like this were possible. Her attraction to him was so intense it felt more like a beautiful, snowy dream than reality.

If she'd known relations between a man and a woman could be like this, maybe she wouldn't have insisted that men weren't for her.

He deepened his kiss and she arched into him, seeking comfort and warmth and a resolution to the unfamiliar pulsing between her legs.

After what felt like hours but was probably closer to minutes, she fought past the lump in her throat and tucked her mussed hair behind her ears. She took a deep breath. "You know how I got so huffy when we were taking off and you asked if I was a virgin?"

"Yeah."

"I practically am."

"As in a haven't-had—you know—virgin?"

She nibbled her lower lip. "Technically, I suppose I'm not a virgin. But that one time… Well, it wasn't very good. I'm not even sure if we did it right."

"If you have to ask," he said with a big, knowing grin, "chances are he fumbled."

"Yeah, that's kinda what I figured."

"So how come you never tried it again?"

She shrugged.

"Been saving yourself for marriage?"

"Not exactly."

"Then why?"

"I don't know. My girlfriends say I expect too much. That I'm looking for perfection in an imperfect world." She bowed her head, thrust her fingers into her long hair and pulled. "Some luck, huh? After all this *saving,* here I am, stranded on a mountaintop and maybe about to—"

"No." He touched his fingers to her lips. "Don't say it. Don't even think it. I mean, I'd be lying if I told you our rescue is guaranteed, but..." He curved his hand to her cheek.

Leaning into his touch, she shivered. He tugged her onto his lap, holding her and kissing her and telling her without a word that whatever happened, at least she wouldn't have to go through it alone.

Her whole life, she'd been alone. Her mom had always had her men. Her dad, his work and various other women. And there she'd been, all on her own, trying to convince herself that that was just the way she liked it. But here, with Colby, she was questioning that. For if going solo was so right, then why did being with Colby feel anything but wrong?

Laughing, she said, "I've never even had an org—well, you know."

"You mean a...oh." He coughed and, thankfully, didn't say the big *O* word out loud.

Good grief, what had gotten into her to even bring it up?

Maybe because the only thing Santa's going to bring me is frostbite?

Sobering, she nodded. "But listen to me, rambling on about something so unimportant in the grand scheme of things. If we don't make it off this mountain, the only person who'll miss me is my landlady—and that's not even because she particularly likes me, but because I'm the only one in the building paid up on my rent." She glanced to her hands, snug in his warm grip, then back into his eyes. "So? Who'll be missing you?"

"Besides my mom..." He squeezed her fingers. "No one special. I don't have a steady girl, or even pets. A lot of great friends, but that's about it." Leaning against his seat, he dropped his head back and sighed. "Mom sent me a plane ticket to fly down to New Mexico for the holidays. She didn't want me flying all that way by myself." With a sad laugh, he added, "What's that old saying about accidents always happening closest to home?"

Whitney swallowed hard. This wasn't happening. *Couldn't* be happening.

On the one hand, she was sharing great conversation with a fun guy. On the other, they might have only hours to live. The very thought didn't seem real, which was probably a good thing, otherwise she'd give in to the acid-tinged panic rising in her throat.

"I feel bad about not going to see her," he said,

gazing out the plane's side window at black fringed with white. "Even in hard times, Christmas was her thing. She always made a point of giving a gift to every single man, woman and child in this town—mostly cookies and homemade candies, but she didn't want anyone feeling alone or left out."

"She sounds like one of those rare souls who truly gets what Christmas is all about."

"Yeah. I miss her. I should've gone down."

"Why didn't you?"

He took his hand back, then used it to rub his forehead. "Long story."

"Unless the Marines show up, I'm not going anywhere."

Colby shot her a look. "I can't believe I'm this petty, but here goes. Truth? I didn't want to see my mom and her new husband because the two of them together—and his three daughters, and their husbands and happy, laughing kids—remind me how much I want to get married and have kids. They make me see what a cool grandmother my mom makes. How much better life would be if I had a family. Hell, seeing all of them makes me feel like less of a man. Like a failure."

"Oh, Colby, no. Not everyone has to get married. That's just what society wants us to think, but—"

"Look," he said, "I don't know about you, but

for me, having my own family isn't about recreating some sentimental magazine photo of a mom, dad and baby around a cozy fireplace. It's about how I feel—or lately, don't—in here." He patted his chest. "Dammit, I wanted a wife. Rug rats. I didn't plan on going out alone."

Whitney bowed her head.

You're not alone, Colby. You have me.

Obviously, though, she wasn't enough, and because it was Christmas Eve and she might not live to see Christmas Day, the realization hurt. Because, maybe for the first time in her life, she wanted more than just her career. That morning, she'd have denied it. But now, with the icy wind howling *now or never,* it was time for honesty—having someone all her own to love didn't sound half bad.

She closed her eyes, trying to find at least momentary relief from the stinging tears that seemed to have taken on a life of their own. After clearing her throat, she said, "You mentioned wanting a wife. Haven't you found the right woman?"

"Thought I had. Margot was up here on vacation. Her father's a Global Oil exec. It was a whirlwind thing. At the end of her two weeks, I asked her to stay. She asked me to come with her. Neither of us bent. End of story."

"I'm sorry," she said.

"Yeah, me, too. Now, I only date local girls."

"Are there many?"

''Sadly, no.''

At another time, in another place, she might have found his comment funny. Now, it only seemed sad. Even in the short time she'd known him, Colby had struck her as a great guy. He deserved a great woman.

Like me.

The crazy thought hit as unexpectedly as the freak storm that had shot down their plane. But was the idea really so wrong?

Wouldn't it be just her stupid luck to meet the man of her dreams just before—

''What're you thinking?'' Colby asked, illuminating her with the flashlight. ''You've got a dangerous look in those big brown eyes.''

She licked her lips. ''My idea is only dangerous if we get rescued. But since you said yourself we probably won't—and you are the local expert in these matters—then...'' She took the light from him and set it on a box that had gotten wedged behind her seat. Aimed outside, it gave the menacing snow an ironically romantic blue glow. Reaching for Colby's hands, she brushed the pads of her thumbs over the soft web between his thumb and forefinger. His skin felt rough but warm. So blessedly warm.

''Oh no,'' he said. ''You're not suggesting what I think you are?''

She nodded. ''Please, Colby. I might not even

get to live, let alone reach my destination. Please don't let me die alone. Even if it's for just one night, I want to feel…'' Out of her mind with fear, guilt, need and doubt, she kissed him, stopping only to slip off her heavy boots and scramble onto his lap. ''Please,'' she said, ringing kisses around the small strip of skin above his sandy-colored wool sweater.

''Whitney…'' Colby closed his eyes and sighed. This couldn't be happening—even though he had, very unprofessionally, been wishing it would. Hands lightly on her shoulders, urging her back, he said, ''From what you've told me, maybe you are still a virgin. And we *are* going to survive. I can't in good conscience take that kind of gift from you. It wouldn't be right. You deserve better than this. A nice, soft bed and candles and romantic music and flowers and wine. I mean, here…the sheer logistics make it—''

She cut him off with another kiss—a seemingly innocent pressing of her soft, bubble-gum-flavored lips to his.

Initially, their lips were cold. Then came a torturous heat Colby knew he wasn't gentlemanly enough to deny.

He might be knocking on death's door, but until then, he was going to live.

Whitney groaned, words caught in her throat. Her pilot—her granter of last wishes—slipped his cool fingers beneath layers of wool and corduroy and cotton until he reached her warm satin bra. He circled his hand over her nipple, honing it into a sensation-filled bud.

Normally, with most men, this was about the point when she called it quits. It wasn't that she was a prude. She just never felt anything. But this time, here with Colby, her world was being transformed from an eight-color box of Crayolas into the giant sixty-four pack with the built-in sharpener.

Hand still teasing her breast, he dragged his lips from her mouth to her neck. Her toes curled with naughty pleasure. She closed her eyes, drawing him even closer.

"Wait." He pulled back again. "If we're going to do this, you should at least be comfortable."

After one more kiss, he gently coaxed her back into her own seat. Then he scrambled into the cargo area, rearranging her luggage and snacks to make room for a makeshift bed. Nestled between her suitcases was her down sleeping bag. He had one, too—an FAA requirement for Alaskan winter flying. Between the two of them, they had more than enough down feathers to line a damned cozy nest.

He took off his jacket and shoes. "Nippy in here," he said.

Teeth chattering, she nodded.

"Look at you," he said, clambering to the front.

He took her into his arms, trying to stop her shivering. When that didn't work, he released her and unzipped his coat. Tucking her warm curves against him, pressing her breasts against his chest, he told himself it was all about shared body heat. He fully planned to be a gentleman.

But then Whitney slipped one of her cold little hands up under his sweater, easing it along the wall of his chest. He wasn't sure who initiated the kissing—wasn't sure it even mattered who, so long as it never stopped.

Together they worked at removing each other's many clothes, and together they fell to the sleeping bags, slipping inside where the flannel was at first cold, but then soft and warm against bare skin.

He was half-on, half-off her, one of his legs between hers. She arched against him. "Now…"

Lips on her throat, he shook his head. "Later. *Much* later."

Gently, he swept a fallen lock of hair from her cheek and whispered her name, hoping both actions said quite plainly what his few words hadn't. *Later, much later, I'm going to make your second time— quite possibly, your last time—one you'll never forget.*

Chapter Three

Deep into the night, Colby had lost count of how many times they'd made love. Whitney had drifted into sleep eventually. Without her to distract him, the gravity of their situation hit hard. The air in the plane's cabin was so cold he could see his breath. A fine sheet of frost coated almost every surface. Already, his beloved plane—his most prized possession—was evolving from transport to tomb.

He moved to rub his stubbled jaw, but Whitney was using his right arm as a pillow.

Good Lord, what a night, he thought, giving himself an awkward scratch with his left hand. Whitney was an amazing girl—woman. Under different circumstances, who knew where things might lead?

Funny, when he'd first landed in this snow bowl in the middle of nowhere, all he could think about were the loose ends of his life that would now be forever undone.

And questions. So many questions.

Would his mom be all right? Who would get his stuff, since he'd never gotten around to drawing up a will? Who would fix Nugget's busted toaster or help him serve Christmas breakfast at the lodge? Who would gather old Henry's firewood when the snow got too deep for him to leave his cabin, and who would make sure he remembered his high-blood-pressure medication?

But now, nestled beside the sweetest curves he'd ever had the pleasure of embracing, his mind skipped to more important things. Matters of family and love.

His father had taken off the day before Colby's sixth birthday. Swallowing hard, he remembered his blow-out-the-candles double wish.

I wish Dad would come home.

I wish Mom would stop crying.

Twenty-five years later, his newlywed mom sported a perpetual grin. His first wish hadn't come true, but at this point, Colby didn't even want it to. As far as he was concerned, his old man was a bum. In every way possible—from overachieving in school to running a successful business while finding time to help anyone in need—Colby had strived to become the kind of man his father had never been. A man worthy of respect.

While Colby was growing up, his mom had wai-tressed at Kodiak Lodge. Having lived in Kodiak Gorge all her life, she'd often said she should have known better than to marry an outsider. She'd since married another, though, and become an outsider herself by moving to New Mexico with a retired CEO she'd met when he'd spent a week in Kodiak Gorge fly-fishing.

Colby used to wonder how she stood the desert heat, but right now an eternity of hundred-degree days didn't sound half bad.

As a kid, Colby had vowed that if he had a son someday, he'd never leave as his father had. Course, in light of his current situation, that was a moot point. From the looks of things, his dream of becoming a dad might never come true. Unless...

He glanced at Whitney. *Could* she be pregnant? No, he decided. And since they might both die, he wouldn't want her to be.

She rolled onto her side, snuggling her cheek against the coarse hairs of his chest.

Colby knew he was too rough around the edges for her type, but then that didn't matter much, either.

"Merry Christmas," she mumbled, the heat of her ice-fogged breath arousing him all over again.

"Merry Christmas yourself, Santa Baby. Although it's still dark and I don't know where you flung my watch, so I have no idea if it's really the big day." He kissed the top of her head, loving the clean scent of her shampoo.

"Who cares? With you, I'm guessing any day would be a big day."

"Thanks," he said, twirling a lock of her hair. "So? You ready for one more lesson?"

She grinned. "Sure, but after that, how about breaking for Christmas cookies and cocoa?"

"Sorry. I'm fresh out. But I do have something else you might like."

"HEY, GUYS, OVER HERE! I think I found 'em!" Working in near-whiteout conditions by the light of battery-powered headlamps near the top of Juneau Ridge, Brody Muldoon waved over the rest of his rescue crew. They operated much like volunteer firefighters, answering any nearby call for help. Hell, for that matter, most of them *were* volunteer firefighters.

Colby Davis would've risked his life for any one of them. For half of the adventure-seeking dimwits in Kodiak Gorge, he already had.

Now it was Colby's turn to be rescued, and by God, not a single man on the crew was prepared to even breathe the word *defeat*—let alone admit it.

The wind shifted, blowing enough snow off the tail of Colby's beloved—and now busted—De-Havilland Beaver to validate Brody's hunch.

"Yeah, baby!" he shouted, already using his lightweight shovel to dig out Colby and his passenger. "One more hour and they'd have been buried till spring."

"Think they're alive?" asked Tanner.

"Hope so. Never much cottoned to dead fish in a can—not even packed in oil."

Tanner grimaced. "Love you, Brode. Always the poet."

"Not!" called out Sergei Koyck, one of the founding members of the crew.

"All right," Brody said. "Let's quit the chatter and dig. It's damned cold out here. Once we find Colby and his fare, I can't wait to sink my teeth into that Christmas ham I smelled cooking at the lodge."

Twenty minutes later, the beams from their headlamps cutting weak yellow paths through blowing snow, the four-man crew located the plane's windshield and then dug around to the door. The temperature must've been dropping a few degrees every minute, 'cause Brody felt as if his ice-crusted eyebrows were crinkle fries.

"Got it," he finally said, digging out the handle, then kicking away the remaining snow to yank open the door. It would have been faster to bust a window, but if either Colby or his fare were unconscious just on the other side, Brody didn't want them cut by glass. "Someone wanna give me more light?"

Tanner offered a powerful flashlight from his tool belt.

"Thanks," Brody said, peering into the gloom. At first glance, the plane appeared abandoned, but then he shone the light into the cargo area. "They're here," he called back to the guys, "but I can't tell if they're still alive."

He climbed in, slicing the light through his foggy breath toward the lumpy mound.

No blood. But no signs of movement, either. And no appendages peeking out to at least give him a clue.

Damn, he hoped they weren't already gone. That'd be a really crappy ending to an already crappy day.

He and Colby went way back. Not that he'd go shouting it from the rooftops, but Brody loved Colby like a brother.

Steeling himself for the worst, praying for the best, Brody jerked back the covers to find a sight even more shocking than two dead bodies.

Two very much alive and buck-naked bodies.

Snuggled together cozy as a couple of squirrels all tucked in for winter were Colby and his fare— both in a deep sleep.

Hmm, their ordeal must've been exhausting, all right—in a *good* way!

Colby's fare was a pretty little thing, decked out in nothing but his goofy Santa hat. Judging by the pink tones of their bare skin, both parties looked to be in excellent condition.

Tossing the cover back over the juicy parts, Brody cleared his throat, then shouted, ''Got 'em, boys!''

Tanner popped his head through the open door. ''Colby okay?'' His lips curved into a wide grin. ''Oh heck, yeah. From the looks of it, I'd say he's doing a damned sight better than the rest of us.''

COLBY SAT STRAIGHT UP, cast a sleepy look at his grinning friends, and said, ''Hot damn. The elves put a rescue crew in my stocking.'' He couldn't stop smiling—until he noticed not just his naked chest, but the naked woman beside him.

Whitney.

Sweet, beautiful, innocent, almost virginal Whitney. After the night they'd just shared, she'd officially become an ex-almost-virgin.

Oh, man, he thought, rubbing his stubbled jaw.

Man, oh man.

Never.

Never, in a million, trillion years would his buds let him live this down. They'd hound him till the end of time, at which point they'd follow him straight to hell to start all over again.

Drawing the covers over himself and his still-sleeping companion, Colby groaned.

What had he done? Oh sure, chances were Whitney wasn't pregnant, but what if she were? There'd be no question about his marrying her. He would. Period. No child of his would ever grow up without his or her dad.

But he was putting the cart before the horse. First off, odds were that she wasn't pregnant. And second, even though he was attracted to Whitney, they weren't anywhere ready for a lifelong commitment.

"Yo, Colby?" Brody said. "You two ready to get the hell off this mountain?"

"Yeah," Colby said, putting his hand to his suddenly aching forehead. "Just give us a sec, will ya?"

"Sure thing, bud. Just come on out when you're ready."

After his friend had left, closing the cabin door behind him, Colby said to the warm curves beside him, "Knock, knock? The coast is clear. You still under there?"

The woman he'd just spent the best hours of his life with poked her mussed head out from under the covers. She wasn't smiling.

"You okay?" he asked, smoothing his fingers over her hair, releasing the subtle, clean scent that had driven him wild all night long. Just the silk of her hair against the palm of his hand renewed his hunger for her.

She nodded but wouldn't meet his gaze.

Slipping his fingers beneath her chin, he forced

her to look at him. "Those guys are cool," he said. "They might come off a little rough around the edges, but trust me, not a word of your part in this will ever be mentioned once we get off the mountain."

Nodding, she swallowed hard.

"Hey then, what's wrong? I know being found in the buff was awkward, but sweetie, we're going to live. That's a good thing, right?"

"Yes, of course. It's just that…"

"What?"

"This…us—all of it—was just so out of character for me. Don't get me wrong, I loved it. Being with you. I wouldn't trade what we've just shared for the world. But while on the outside nothing's changed, in here—" She touched her hand to her heart "—I'm scared to death that nothing will ever be the same."

"What do you mean?"

"Beats me," she said with a shy smile. "Maybe just that I thought I had my whole life figured out, but now, I'm not so sure."

"Well, hey," he said, lacing his fingers through hers. "How about letting me help you figure it out? My hours are pretty flexible. Over the next few weeks, we could get to know each other under less stressful circumstances."

"That sounds nice," she said. Her wistful expression squeezed his heart. "But I don't think so."

"Why?"

"It would just never work."

"What wouldn't? I'm not talking lifelong commitment here—just sharing a bottle of wine over a good meal. I'll even cook."

"Thank you," Whitney said. "I appreciate the offer. In fact, I appreciate everything you've done for me. You're a super pilot for getting us through this alive—and an even better friend—but I think that's where it should end."

That's where it has to end, because as incredible as it seems, over the course of one night, I've fallen for you, Colby Davis. Hard. The problem is, what we shared wasn't real. It was a magical night based on the fact that we both thought we were going to die. We both said and did things we never would've under ordinary circumstances. How do I know the man you were last night is the real you? How do I know the feelings you evoked in me were real?

Bottom line, Whitney thought, as she clutched the covers higher around her neck, was that the depth of her feelings for Colby was scary. The easiest way to avoid having to explore those feelings was to ignore them.

She'd return to her world. Colby would return to his. And, with any luck, the two of them would never meet again. As painful as that might be, it was the only sane thing to do.

For very sound reasons, she'd distrusted men for most of her life. Why on earth would she trade that wealth of emotional knowledge for one idyllic night, that under ordinary circumstances, would never have happened?

"Women." Reaching for his shirt, Colby shook his head. "If I live to be a hundred, I'll never understand you people."

Rolling her eyes, she grabbed her own top. "Likewise."

Colby finished dressing in silence, then said, "I'll wait outside for you to get your clothes on—but you might want to hurry. The weather's not getting any better."

"Okay, thanks. Oh—Colby?"

"Yeah?"

"I'm sorry."

"Me, too."

After they'd loaded Whitney's luggage and junk food into Brody's Cessna—he'd put skis on it for the winter—the trip to the Global Oil site took just under an hour.

Dot, the only woman on Global's crew, showed Whitney to her room. A few minutes later, Whitney returned and thanked Colby again, along with the rest of the guys. Then, without so much as a hug, she claimed exhaustion and went to bed.

Beside a roaring fire in Global's rec room, with *Christmas Vacation* blaring on the big screen,

Colby clinked beer bottles with Brody. "Thanks again, man. I wasn't looking forward to becoming a human Popsicle."

Brody cracked a smile. "Didn't look like you were in too much danger of that, judging by the heat you and Miss Chicago were radiating."

"Man…" Colby snorted. "Talk about a failure to communicate. There was one point during the night when I actually thought she could've been the one. I mean, we were…" He shook his head. "Then once you guys got there—poof—it was like the woman I met had been a dream."

"She's a dream, all right," Brody said, sipping his beer. "Definitely too good for the likes of you."

"Thanks, man. Appreciate it."

"You bet." Brody slapped Colby's back. "Just doing my part to keep you real."

WITH THE WIND HOWLING outside her beige cell of a bedroom, Whitney tried losing herself to sleep, but it refused to come. Over and over her mind kept flashing back to Colby and the wonderfully wild time they'd shared.

She closed her eyes and caught glimpses of him freeze-framed in her own private movie. His square-jawed face and sea-green eyes. Those biceps and washboard abs. She'd loved just staring at him and running her fingers along his rippled stomach and the tree trunks he called arms. He'd probably earned his strength by chopping wood and maintaining his plane—the one now stuck forever at the top of a mountain.

What would he do without it? Undoubtedly, he had insurance. But still, having been through one minor auto accident that had required her to submit a claim, she knew the next few weeks didn't hold much fun for him.

Her throat tightened.

In a perfect world, she'd want to be there with him, helping him through his frustration. But if there was one thing she'd learned in her twenty-six years, it was that as beautiful as the world often was, it could also be cruel.

Her own parents—even friends with failed relationships—had shown her that a girl like her would be playing with dynamite to entertain, even for a second, the notion of staying with Colby.

In the first place, how did she know he'd even want her to stay? And in the second, she *couldn't* stay.

I'm afraid of falling for him. Of opening myself up—I could get hurt. And what about my career? I've worked so hard to get where I am.

She curled onto her side beneath a pile of wool blankets and hugged Colby's Santa hat, which still smelled of him. Lulled by off-key carols and the faint male laughter drifting in from the rec room, she felt drowsiness overtake her. From the sound of things, quite a few guys were still awake. It wasn't any old masculine voice catching her attention, though. Only Colby's.

Had it really been less than twelve hours since all his laughs had been for her?

Squeezing her eyes tight, for what she promised herself would be the last time, she imagined herself with him. Maybe in Global's festive rec room? Or that cozy cabin of his he'd talked about? Shoot, since it was her fantasy, she even tried imagining him in her ultra-feminine Chicago apartment. But try as she might, she just couldn't see brawny Colby Davis at home on her turf.

No, he belonged up here in the wild. Alaska suited him. Just as she knew deep in her heart that it didn't suit her.

With a sigh, she returned to her fantasy of Colby's cabin. She was back in front of a crackling fire, back in the circle of his arms. They'd share a few beers, a few jokes, a few still-warm Christmas cookies, and most of all…a few more spellbinding kisses.

"WELL, GUESS THIS IS IT," Colby said to Whitney well over a month later in mid-February, not sure what else to say in the few minutes before she had to go through security and board her commercial flight. When she'd called and asked him, in a painfully polite voice, to fly her from the oil site to

Anchorage, he'd agreed—against his better judgment. After picking her up in a rented Aviat, he'd spent an awkward couple of hours trying his damnedest not to brush his arms against hers or to inhale the familiar scent of her shampoo.

At the Anchorage airport, she hadn't wanted him to escort her to the security gates, but he'd insisted, needing to make sure she made the short trip safely.

His conscience twinged.

Yeah, right, what he really needed to do was make sure she once and for all left him in peace.

With her finally back in Chicago, he wouldn't have to worry so much about his downright spooky attraction to her. That attraction had done its fair share of keeping him up late at night, dreaming of her. Of the sexy cinch of her waist easing into lush hips, of the rush of tenderness that swept through him when he just whispered her name.

''Thanks,'' she said, pausing in front of the metal detectors to hold out her right hand for him to shake.

He took her slight hand in his and gulped.

How could one simple touch bring back so many steamy memories?

The smoothness of her skin. The heat of her breath on his lips just before he kissed her. The heavy swell of her warm breasts in his hands as her nipples hardened against his palms.

He shook his head. This had to stop.

For whatever reason, the lady didn't have the hots for him like he had for her—or, correction, *had* had. His momma didn't raise no fool. Ever since Whitney had given him the cold shoulder the night of their rescue, he'd warned himself to stop thinking about her. And the instant she set foot on her flight, forgetting her would be a whole lot easier.

She'd be back in Chicago. He'd be back at work. And with any luck, he'd never, *ever,* have to see her again.

"Thanks for what?" he managed to ask, barely able to breathe through the storm of emotions crashing through him. What was wrong with him? Why couldn't his body take the hint that no matter how good the two of them had once been, whatever chemistry they'd shared was over?

She shrugged before turning his insides to mush with the sweetest, saddest grin.

Were those tears shimmering in her eyes?

She swallowed hard. "Thanks for just being you, Colby Davis."

For a second, he thought she was going to follow that cryptic statement with a hug, but she didn't. A guy in a fancy suit gruffly asked if he could cut past her in line. And just like that, the moment was gone, and so was she.

Watching her slight form disappear among the

other travelers crowding the concourse, Colby tucked his hands into his jeans pockets, then muttered, "Goodbye, Whitney." Finally he turned away from her and headed back to his life.

Chapter Four

Colby used the tail of his red flannel shirt to wipe sweat from his abs, but then figured, what the hell? Days like this were a gift from the Alaskan gods, so he went ahead and took his shirt off, tossing it onto the dock. The hot July sun warmed his chest as he buffed the left wing of his new girl, Janine— a 1999 Cessna Caravan he'd gotten an outrageous deal on due to the previous owner's divorce.

Reason? The usual. Poor guy's wife hated Alaska.

Hated eternal sun and bugs in summer, eternal darkness and snow in winter.

Too bad she hadn't stuck around to see today.

Not a cloud within five hundred miles. A hint of a breeze sighing through the spruce, stirring the lake just enough to shoot diamonds off choppy waves lapping the underside of the stubby dock.

And the smell.

Sweet holy Mary, there was nothing quite like

the smell of Kodiak Lake baking in the sun. The musky, mossy, fishy blend made his mouth water just thinking about all those trout he planned on catching next weekend. Of course, since today was Saturday, his much-anticipated weekend off was still another whole week away. He put his back into buffing the finish his new owner's manual called Jet-Glo Snow White.

From across the lake flashed a glint of white sun on glass. A dust cloud billowed behind a fast-moving red pickup. Henry. With luck, he was delivering that box of reworked parts Colby was supposed to fly out to the Global Oil site this afternoon.

Kneeling to slap the lid on his can of wax, Colby eased his lips into a smile. It was good to be back in his routine. Transporting tourists to the best fishing spots. Bringing supplies and mail to the Global site and to the smattering of Kodiak Gorge citizens who lived on the edge of civilization but still had an occasional hankering to read the *Miami Sun Herald* or eat Virginia ham.

Back on his feet, heading for his office, Colby noted that Henry was nearly there—not that the chug-glugging of his cantankerous old Ford hadn't already announced that fact. Every winter, Henry tucked the truck into his shed till spring. And every spring there were bets on whether or not the heap would start back up.

This particular winter being so harsh, Colby had been among those betting that this would be the year the old truck finally gave up the ghost. But to the contrary, much like Henry himself, it had come back louder and smellier than ever. Smoking and belching, the vehicle startled a flock of geese into honking flight as it rounded the swampy area at the lake's south end.

Colby grinned.

Yep, it'd been a long winter, but summer had finally come, along with an end to all his waiting.

Waiting for insurance money to come through. Waiting for his mom to stop calling every day to make sure he was okay. Waiting to find a new plane. Worst of all, waiting for the guys around town to lay off with the wolf whistles every time he strode into sight.

Okay, so he'd been caught with his pants down, but it wasn't like ninety percent of the gang hanging out at Kodiak Lodge wouldn't have done the same had they been stuck in a similar situation.

After all, Whitney was beautiful, intelligent and funny. She had the most luxurious black hair, and her nose crinkled when she laughed. And those eyes—big and brown—were shot with intriguing amber flecks even his dim flashlight had picked up.

After the guys had rescued them, she'd had about the same initial reaction he'd had—jubilation at first, then embarrassment, then shock. In the hour

MANAGER BETH PEA
(765) 284 - 7181

ST# 1665 OP# 00002731 TE# 09 TR# 08363
LAY S   002840004059   2.96 N
EPSON SALT   0684113168763   1.94 X
MICH ENTREE   071786410716   1.50 O
WAYNE JIMMY   060044503552   9.72 X
GV CAPPUCIN   060538818710   1.96 O
YOP CUST BLK   007047000135   0.80 O
RX VITAMINS   030122000817   3.96 X
SNAPPLE   00760816859   0.98 X
YOP LT CHERY   00704700066   0.50 O
ROMANCE   00653730600   8.99 X
ROMANCE   00653383007   4.20 X
ROMANCE   00653
ROMANCE   00653
WOMANS WORLD
ROMANCE   00653
WALMART ALE   00704
PARTYWARE   017
FRIGO STR   021
FRIGO STR   045
FRIGO   CR   004
FRIGO   CR   004

                 SUBTOTAL

                 TOTAL
                 DEBIT TEND
                 CHANGE DUE

EFT DEBIT   PAY FROM PRIMARY
ACCOUNT   31.50
     US   TOTAL PURCHASE
REF # 431040009
NETWORK ID. 0062 APPR CODE 480006
        11/06/04   02:19:2

ITEMS SOLD 21

TC# 0431 7340 0763 1453

Shrek 2-VHS/DVD
available Friday Nov
11/06/04   02:19:30

it had taken to deliver her and all her junk food to the oil site, they'd said a whole five words.

She'd chosen a seat well away from him on Brody's plane, making it painfully clear that what they'd shared—whatever it was—wasn't only over, but that it never should've happened. That only made him grumpier, since she was the one who'd practically begged him not to let her die an almost-virgin.

When he'd left her at the airport, he'd felt as though the least he should do was wish her well with a friendly hug, but she'd stood ramrod-stiff.

Lucky for him, he reminded himself with a sharp breath, was the fact that she was thousands of miles away from him and presumably busy with her Chicago life. Right where she belonged. Right where, though he'd never admit it, he hoped she'd stay. Not that he'd given their encounter much thought.

After all, it had just been a night. An ordinary night. Crash a plane. Make love five or six times. Nothing too earth-shattering there.

Oh, yeah? Then why was he getting hard just thinking about her? Not to mention his last time seeing her?

HENRY BLARED the red Ford's horn, jolting Colby from his downright unacceptable memories. Fanning himself with a box flap, he blamed the day's sunshine for dredging up all that heat.

Shrouded in a cloud of dust, the truck stopped a mere two feet from the lake's edge. The sun's glare on the Ford's tinted windows prevented Colby from seeing most of the car's interior. "How're things?" Henry shouted out the open driver's side window with a wave of his beat-up fedora.

"Couldn't be better." Colby set his box filled with waxing supplies on a dock post. "Been to the clinic yet about your arthritis?"

Henry shooed off the question.

"You do know they have medicine to help?"

"Damned horse pills. Save your mothering for someone who needs it."

Colby grinned. Looked like he'd be taking Henry to the doctor himself. "You bring those parts for Global?"

"What parts?" Henry turned off the engine, then eased open his door.

The geese that had only just settled down about a quarter mile down the road started honking again.

"What do you mean, what parts?" Colby asked, shrugging into his shirt. "Global hired you to re-work them two weeks ago. You promised to have them to me no later than today—coincidentally, the same day I promised them to Global."

Henry waved him off. "What I brought is way more fun than some old parts. Got dropped off at the lodge last night. Think that fella Vic, out of Anchorage, was the one making the delivery."

"Oh yeah?" Hand to his forehead, shading his eyes from the glare, Colby said, "Unless you happen to have a million bucks stashed in there with my name on it, I'd just as soon have Global's parts."

Henry turned to the truck and hollered, "You ever plannin' on getting out?"

The squeal of the rusty passenger door sent the geese into such a commotion that they took off for the far end of the lake.

"Come on over," Henry shouted. "I promise Colby won't bite."

WON'T BITE?

Actually, now that Whitney had a second to think about it, yes, Colby had taken a few lusty nips that steamy December night. Not that she'd thought about their time together since then—unless, of course, those thoughts concerned her current situation. And in that case, thinking of him was not only understandable, but advisable.

To a certain extent.

Forcing a deep breath, tucking her long hair neatly behind her shoulders, she pushed her considerable mass off the truck's seat and onto the ground, trying to be swanlike but feeling more like a one-legged loon.

She took her time stepping out from the shield of the truck's door, unprepared for the impact of what seeing Colby again might do to her—and what his seeing her might do to him.

Sooner than she would've liked, she was struggling to conquer her runaway heart and sweating palms. And all because Colby Davis stood backdropped by a blazing blue sky, looking way better than any mental image she'd ever even dreamed of conjuring up.

Tall and lean and tan and…oh my.

She licked her lips, willing her fingertips to stop tingling as she remembered running then up and down his abs.

Forcing her gaze higher, she landed in serious trouble. Trouble tinted Gulf of Alaska green. He was staring at her as though, rather than your average *very* pregnant woman, she was a creature beamed down from a galaxy far, far away.

Easing her lips into a smile, she said, "Um, hi, Colby. Long time no see, huh?"

He grinned as if laughing at a private joke, then shook his head, looking down while kicking the gravel at his feet.

She took a few tentative steps forward, left hand on her seven-month-pregnant stomach, the other smoothing windswept hair off her cheek to tuck it behind her ear. "How have you been?"

"Oh, no," he said, taking equal steps back, warding her off with outstretched hands. "Don't tell me I'm—I mean, we, I mean—" There again went that brilliant, white-toothed smile. The one she'd replayed a thousand times in her head—strictly for informational purposes. After all, she did need to periodically apprise herself of her unborn child's future dental health. "Wow. Guess I'm not quite sure what I mean. I mean, of course, I must be your baby's…why else would you be here?"

Whitney turned to Henry. "You can go ahead and leave. Looks like this might take a while."

"You sure?" the wiry old guy said. "I don't mind stayin'. This here's way better than anything happening on my soaps."

Whitney felt silly for having to swallow back tears.

What had she expected? Harps playing in the trees and little blue booties falling from heaven upon her arrival?

It wasn't as if she'd returned to Kodiak Gorge looking for a husband, or even a father for her child. All she'd wanted to do before she got too far along to travel was inform Colby that he was going to be a dad.

Period.

He could handle the news as he pleased—just as long as beyond developing a mutually agreeable visitation schedule, his actions had nothing to do with her or what ultrasounds promised was her son.

After all, she'd determined around about her

mom's fifth wedding that marriage would never be for her. And now that her career was going strong, Whitney was entirely self-sufficient.

Sure, it would take some adjustment to fit a baby into her hectic schedule, but that was okay. She'd already interviewed several excellent nannies, and once Talbot Livingston Foster II—she'd decided to name him after her mother's father—got old enough, he could happily spend his toddlerhood at her company's in-house day care. It was top-notch.

Whitney parked herself on a rough-hewn log bench paralleling the dock while Colby followed Henry to his truck, mumbled a few choice-sounding yet unintelligible phrases, then just stood there, hands in his pockets, watching his friend drive off.

He turned back to her just as a breeze whipped up off the lake, catching the flaps of the box sitting on a dock post.

By the time it occurred to Whitney that the box didn't look all that stable, it'd already tumbled into the water.

"Oops," Whitney mumbled, looking forward to the day when her reactions once again matched her thoughts. As efficiently as possible, she pushed herself off the bench and knelt on the edge of the dock, hoping to snatch one of the flaps before the whole thing sank.

"Here, let me get it," Colby said, jogging onto the dock.

He beat her to the box, but just as he grabbed it, she grabbed it. Before she could find her center of gravity, she'd begun a free fall into the water.

A screech prefaced her splash, and while she wasn't at risk of drowning because she knew perfectly well how to swim, she was shocked by the water's icy chill.

A second later came another splash, as Colby jumped in after her, which was ludicrous, since she'd only landed in water barely up to her neck. Still, when he wrapped his arms around her to tow her to shore, she didn't complain.

"Thanks," she said as he helped her slosh onto the grass, the padded insoles of her black pumps squishing. A picnic table sat beside a boulder that had bright blue forget-me-nots blooming from every crack and crevice. "T-t-hat's p-pretty," she said, teeth already chattering.

Colby unfastened his jeans to reveal black boxers dotted with gray airplanes.

"W-what are you d-doing?" she asked.

"What's it look like I'm doing? Taking off these jeans so I can go inside and put on new ones. You're doing the same with that uptight business suit."

"Really, Colby, I'm fine. It's such a nice day. I'll just dry off in the s-sun."

He shot her stomach a look. "We made…a baby

together, and now you're worried about me seeing some skin?''

''The baby—it's a boy.''

Looking to the sky, he swiped his fingers through the glistening spikes of his hair, then shook his head while his face erupted in a huge smile. ''A son? I'm having a son?''

''Well…to be technical, *I'm* having a son.'' She grinned.

''Sure, but me, too. Wow. At first I was—hell, I mean heck, I didn't know what I was feeling. But to think that inside you is a little kid with maybe my momma's eyes and my cravings for flapjacks with extra butter and syrup, and my love of basketball, and—'' He looked to where she stood shivering by the water's edge. ''Would you listen to me,'' he said, ''rambling on like a gossipy old woman when you and my son are standing there freezing? Come on, woman, take off those clothes.''

''I don't think so.''

''Oh, come on, it's not as if we haven't seen each other before. By the end of the day we'll be walking down the aisle together. Don't turn prude on me now.''

''Considering how bossy you've become, I wouldn't walk down the road with you, let alone any aisles!'' She shivered, at which point he took the matter out of her hands by scooping her off her feet and into his arms. "What are you doing?" she shouted.

"Getting my son into a hot shower."

IN THE GLORIFIED toolshed-turned-office where Colby occasionally crashed after returning from late flights, he found Whitney a new outfit, complete with thick white socks. He offered her a pair of dry boxers, but she'd politely declined before locking herself in the bathroom.

Dressed in dry jeans and a green Kodiak Lodge T-shirt, Colby sat on a stool at the counter of his kitchenette, glowering toward the tiny bathroom.

The shower went off, and in his mind's eye he saw her all steamy and fresh-scrubbed, breasts full, stomach ripe with his son.

His son!

He couldn't wait to teach his kid to fly and fish and play ice hockey and—well, granted he'd have to get the kid out of diapers before trying any of that, but now that Whitney was moving back, there'd be plenty of time to hash out the already bustling schedule of his son's life.

The bathroom door opened, and his future bride moved into the triangle of light spilling through, looking better than he ever had in a pair of his gray sweatpants and a navy-blue T-shirt with a big bulge in the middle. She'd towel-dried her long hair and the inky spirals left the T-shirt's shoulders damp.

Even from this distance, he could tell she looked tired, so he got up from his stool and guided her to the recliner he kept in front of an old black-and-white TV that on sunny days picked up one channel.

"I can walk, you know," she said in a voice as chilly as the lake.

"Yeah. You also get an A plus in cranky."

"Sorry," she said, expression sincere. "I'm hungry—and I left my suitcase of snacks back at the lodge."

He laughed.

"What?"

"You and your snacks. I'll be sure to stock up for you by the time you get to my house."

Fingering her hair, she said, "What do you mean, get to your house? For the next week, I'll be perfectly fine at the lodge." She paused. "I never planned to stay that long but the airfare was much cheaper."

"Sure, you'll be fine," he said, reaching into a cabinet for a box of crackers and a can of squirt cheese. "For tonight, anyway. I imagine it'll take at least that long to get a marriage license, but by tomorrow night you'll be living with me."

"Excuse me?" She froze.

He held out her goodies. "What don't you understand?"

"How about every word out of your mouth?" she said as she took the food items.

He reached for the recliner's side handle and flung her back, causing her to cry, "Colby!"

"Sorry. You shouldn't be on your feet."

"I'm not. In case you've suddenly gone blind as well as crazy, I was already sitting down."

"Yeah, but you should be lying down, after falling in the water and traveling and all."

She sighed.

"Oh, hey, give me those," he said, snatching back the crackers and cheese. "Where are my manners?" In seconds, he'd prepared three crackers, each piled with a perfect spiral of cheese. He held one to her lips. "Eat."

He could tell her first instinct was to bat his hand away, but evidently hunger got the best of her as she jumped at his bait like a rainbow trout after one of his best flies.

"Thankwou," she said around chewing. She swallowed, then nailed him with an amber-flecked glare. "Colby, as nice as all this invalid treatment is, you do understand I'm pregnant and not dying?"

He shrugged. "As far as I'm concerned, I've missed enough of my son's life. I'm not going to miss a second more." *My dad left me and I'll be damned if I let anything get between me and my boy—even his mom.*

"Yes, well." She dropped her gaze. "That's just it. You seem to be under the impression that you have a choice in the matter, and the fact is, you don't."

Chapter Five

Colby blinked. "Okay, let me recap. You show up, seven months' pregnant by my calculations, then tell me it's my baby. I'm cool with that. Granted, it's a shock, but the more I think about it, the more I figure the three of us are going to lead a great life."

"True—only we'll be leading those lives apart."

He frowned. "Come again?"

"Baby Talbot and I, we'll be in Chicago, while you'll be—*ooh!*" Her cheeks took on a flushed glow, and her eyes sparkled.

"What?" he said, on his knees beside her. "Are you all right? Does bickering hurt the baby?"

She grinned and took the other two crackers from his open palm, popping one into her mouth and setting the other on her chest. Then she reached for his hand, curving his fingers around the peak of what he'd already dubbed Mt. St. Nick in honor of the fact that the little guy had been conceived on a mountain on Christmas Eve. "What?" he asked again.

"Shh," she said. "Feel."

"Whoa!" Tears sprang to Colby's eyes. "Was that what I think it was?"

She nodded. "That's my son."

"Don't you mean *our* son?"

"Well, technicallwy," she said around the last cracker. "But here's the deal. I didn't come here wanting anything from you. I just thought you might want to know you're going to be a father."

"And the thought never occurred to you that I might want to do more for my kid than send him a few postcards of grizzlies and the Northern Lights?"

She wriggled her sock-clad toes.

He reached for her chin, gently turning her to face him. "Answer me."

"I can't."

"Why not?"

"Because the idea of you being a full-time dad is so far outside of the realm of possibility it never even crossed my mind. I mean, I've reserved a nanny, and a slot in my company's day care, and…"

Her tone implied that since she already had all of those logistics worked out, her son didn't even need a dad.

Colby took a deep breath.

Maybe he was going about this all wrong. He'd never liked being told what to do. Could he blame Whitney if she didn't, either?

Taking her hands in his, he said, "I'm sorry if it seemed like I was ramrodding my agenda down your throat, but work with me here. You've had seven months to adjust to this and I've had about twenty minutes. I just, well, I assumed you were here to get married."

"I can see where you would," she said, "and I suppose in the case of other women, you'd be right in that assumption, but…" She blinked fast a couple of times. "The whole marriage thing—it's just not for me. Besides which, there's my job to consider. Not to mention the not-so-little matter of us practically being strangers. Anyway, sorry I snapped at you. After my snack, I'm feeling much calmer."

"Good," he said, nodding while patting her stomach, hoping for another feel of his wriggling son. "Calm is good. Okay, so here's my take on the matter…. No son of mine is growing up without his father."

While she'd been in the shower, he'd scoured the place for an engagement ring, but the only thing he'd come up with was a large nut—the metal kind, not a walnut or pecan. He fumbled getting it out of his jeans pocket.

Clink. It hit the hardwood floor before rolling beneath Whitney's chair.

Colby groaned.

She peered over the edge of her seat and said, "Look, if you're about to do what I think you're about to do, you might as well save your breath."

Grunting, he shoved her chair a good fifteen inches back, causing her to exclaim yet again.

When the chair lurched, she grabbed the top of his head, but her pulling his hair didn't hurt—at least not physically. Emotionally, though, it reminded him of *that* night, and the way she'd plunged her fingers into his hair every time he'd brought her to—

"Found it," he said, wishing he could as easily find a fix for the fire raging beneath his fly.

He blew on the ring, buffed it across his T-shirt to make sure it had a sort of pretty shine. Since he was already on his knees, he figured at least that "down on bended knee" thing was taken care of. He cleared his throat, then reached for Whitney's left hand, but she'd already clenched it into a fist.

"Come on," he complained. "How am I supposed to propose if you won't even let me see your ring finger?"

"Simple. You're not proposing. I already told you I didn't come up here to find a husband, but solely to fulfill my moral obligation and offer visitation rights."

At that, he had to laugh. "Oh, and you don't think you have a moral obligation to see to it your baby grows up in a loving, two-parent home?"

"Who said anything about love? All I see is some guy on his knees, holding up…what is that thing?"

"A nut. And so you're turning me down just because I'm not offering a three-carat rock?"

"No. Not at all. I'm turning you down for one reason."

"Okay, let's hear it."

"I'm *never* getting married. Please understand— it's nothing personal. You're a great guy. But I made the decision a long time ago and I plan to stick to it." Not only had her own parents proved an excellent case study to back up her choice, but so had countless friends with their failed marriages and relationships. And if those weren't enough, she'd also read hundreds of work-related files on divorce.

Colby needed to face facts.

No matter how romanticized marriage had become in their society, Whitney believed the concept of a man and woman living happily ever after was as rare as siblings without rivalry.

"Yeah, well, I can be just as bullheaded, and I say we *are* getting married."

"Aren't."

"Are."

"Aren'—"

He stopped the mother of his son midprotest with the mother of all kisses. At first, she stiffened, but then he slipped his hand beneath her tangled, still-damp hair. That only made him want more, so he moved closer, close enough that he was almost sharing the recliner with her. But then baby Nick was getting in the way, so Colby had to finagle himself into an even more awkward position. The recliner lurched, squeaking and creaking before shattering into a half-dozen splintered sections.

"Colby!" Whitney laughed. "Are you trying to kill us?"

"Nope," he said, drawing her into another kiss. "I was just trying to create a good excuse for putting a recliner at the top of our list when we register for wedding gifts down at Schlump's Hardware, Furniture and Jewelry."

"Mmm," Whitney said, popping the last bite of prime rib sandwich into her mouth. Sensing a stalemate back at Colby's so-called office, she'd convinced him to return her to Kodiak Lodge.

While he'd waited for their dinner order to arrive, she'd waddled upstairs to smooth her hair into a crude French twist, then change into business attire. The straight-lined black dress, flats and hose had fit better when she'd been at five months, but the scratchy linen blend made her feel more in control than she'd felt cocooned in the soft cotton and all-too-familiar scents of Colby's sweats.

"Now see?" she said, finishing off her garlic toast. "Doesn't a nice hot meal make everything better?"

Colby grunted.

"What's that supposed to mean?" she asked, fanning herself while moving her chair back from the crackling fire. Granted, it was a little chilly outside, but this was ridiculous.

"You hot?"

She nodded.

He frowned, got up, grabbed her milk and plate, and set them on a table beside the long bank of picture windows overlooking the sun-kissed lake. When she made no move to get up, he said, "Want me to carry you?"

Rolling her eyes, she struggled to her feet, then crossed to the new table. After taking her seat, she gulped her milk and wished it was a large, caffeine-laden Mountain Dew.

Nugget, the lodge's owner, must've eyed them through the kitchen pass-through. Big as a lumberjack and wielding a meat cleaver as efficiently as any ax, he ambled their way, his expression as fiery as his red hair. "What's the problem?" he asked. "Don't like that table?"

"She's hot," Colby said.

"You gonna clean both messes?"

"If it's a problem," Whitney said, "I can move back." She snatched a menu from between the salt-and-pepper shakers to use as a fan.

"Ladybug." Nugget placed his meaty hand on Whitney's shoulder. "It's not a problem for you—just him. Oh, here, let me refill this for you. A woman in your condition can never drink too much milk." He shot Colby a look, then snatched Whitney's empty glass, returning with it full to the brim.

"All right…" Colby sighed, eased back in his chair and crossed his arms. "Let's have it, Nugget. What's in your craw?"

The lodge owner eyed him a good long while with a merciless beady blue stare. "You wanna know what's in my craw, Colby Davis? Then I suggest you head on down to the library and bone up on the Kodiak Gorge history of deadbeat dads."

Colby pressed his lips tight.

It wasn't like Nugget to play dirty. Obviously with that deadbeat dad reference, he was referring to Colby's own dad—how he'd up and deserted his wife and son. Yeah, Colby could've let Nugget in on the truth of the matter—that he was all set to marry Whitney, only she wouldn't have him. But what was the point in explaining, seeing how until he put a ring on her finger, everyone in town seemed hell-bent on thinking the worst of him?

Nugget all but growled before stalking back to his lair.

"What was that all about?" Whitney asked, leaning forward as much as Baby Talbot would allow.

"Take a wild guess."

"I wouldn't have a clue."

He snorted.

"What? How am I supposed to know?"

He leaned forward, too, enough so that the lingering scents of prime rib and sour cream combined with the scents that on that long-ago snowy night, she'd come to know as him. Sweat. Leather. Airplanes, and the sexy speed that they implied.

It took her a second to regroup before she'd even realized he'd been talking. "Excuse me?" she said.

"What part about the fact that my good friend Nugget thinks I'm a world-class jerk didn't you understand?"

"All of it." She smiled.

Leaning back, he sighed. "Look, he obviously thinks what any other sane person—including me—would. That the only reason you came back here was to claim a husband for you, and a father for your baby. And rightly so. Hell—I mean—heck, I'm prepared to make an honest woman of you just as soon as we can get the license, but—"

"But I'm being stubborn as a big ole Alaska-sized mule, right?" She'd adopted what she hoped was an appropriate back-country twang.

"This isn't a joke, Whitney. We're talking about a child here—*my* child."

"Correction—*my* child."

"Okay," Colby said, easing back in his chair. "For the sake of the argument, let's agree to address Nick as *our* child."

"Fine. Only his name is going to be Talbot."

"Over my dead and bloated body."

"Mmm…that's a mighty tempting proposition that I—" She leaned forward to add emphasis to her upcoming point.

Splash!

Whitney's freshly poured milk tipped, sloshing all over her and the table and the floor and her dress and—

"You were saying?" Colby flashed her a grin.

"Here's napkins," Nugget called out as he hustled from the kitchen. To Colby, he added, "What're you doing just sitting there, you big oaf? Can't you see the lady needs help?"

The trio of men who'd been sitting in the corner eating burgers also leapt to her assistance. "Let me help, ma'am," the biggest said.

"I'll help her, Stanley," Colby said, pushing back his chair, napkin in hand. He parted the crowd to pat Whitney's soaking lap. "After all, she is about to be my wife."

"Then you already asked her to marry you?" Nugget asked, releasing a gush of air. "Thank heavens. I was afraid you'd taken the same path as that no 'count—''

''I'm not,'' Colby said, cutting Nugget off. It wasn't anyone's business but his own what his father had done. Continuing with his task, he ran the napkin across regions of Whitney's lap he hadn't touched since...

He looked up just in time to see her cheeks glow.

''In fact,'' he said, dabbing the soggy napkin up her inner thigh, ''for the past hour we've been hammering out the details of our upcoming ceremony, haven't we, sweetie?'' His lowered tone, gritted teeth, and squeeze to her knee implied that, for whatever reason, he wanted her to play along with his delusion, but Whitney was having none of it.

''No, *sweetie,* if you'd ever stop arguing long enough to listen to reason, you'd have heard me patiently explain that in today's society—''

Lips pressed into a dangerously thin line, right in the middle of her latest speech, Colby slapped the sodden napkin to her almost-empty plate, then stormed out of the lodge. And hey, she'd still had a baked potato skin left that she'd been planning to dip in ketchup!

How dare he not only ruin her potato, but walk out on her like that? Leaving her alone with four gaping strangers *and* the bill.

''You really oughta marry 'im,'' said a squat man with a big red nose and even bigger black cowboy hat. "Elsewise, there'll be no livin' with him."

The burly guy Colby had called Stanley removed his worn brown UPS hat to swat the shorter guy on the back of his head. "Damn straight there'll be no livin' with him. Colby'll move to wherever she lives."

"What if that's Texas? You know how he hates Texas."

"Well, then, he'll just have to deal with it when the time comes."

"Yeah, well, what if she's from some fool place like California, huh? Then what's he gonna—"

The graying man, who up to this point had stayed out of it, dropped to one knee in front of Whitney, removing his Kodiak Gorge Auto Repair ball cap to tuck it beneath his left arm. "Ma'am," he said, boldly grasping her hand, "if Colby out there won't marry you, I will."

Nugget started swatting all three of them with the dishrag he'd brought in from the kitchen. "Oh, hush up and leave her alone. For pity's sake. You'd think none of you'd ever seen a woman before."

"None pretty as her," the graying man said.

To Whitney, Nugget said, "Go on upstairs and change. We'll see about cleaning up this mess."

"Thanks, but no," Whitney said, swishing yet another napkin through the largest white puddle. "I can't let you do all of this." She tried getting up, but her belly caught the edge of the table, shifting it just enough to knock the ketchup bottle onto the polished wood floor. "I'm so sorry," she said, cheeks warm. "The baby's growing so fast. I guess I'm not used to being so big."

All four of them had stopped bickering to stare. "What?" Whitney asked.

Nugget shook his head. "You need looking after."

Now it was Whitney's turn to thrust back her shoulders. Looking after? The man acted like she was a child, instead of about to have her own child. "I'll have you know I've been self-sufficient for quite some time now—not to mention the fact that I graduated in the top two percent of my college class."

Laughing, Nugget said, "That's book smarts. What I'm talkin' about is common sense. The kind of sense that if you had even a smidgen of, you'd be using to run right out that door and ask Colby to marry you."

"But I barely even know him," Whitney explained. "We live thousands of miles apart." *Besides which, I'm doing just fine on my own, thank you very much, which is why no matter how sweet or handsome or determined to marry me Colby happens to be, I'll never marry him—or any man.* "Why would we even want to get married?"

The three stooges gravely shook their heads and turned back to their table.

With one last snort, Nugget pushed through the swinging kitchen door.

AFTER NUGGET SHOOED her out of the dining room, Whitney trudged upstairs to change from her stained dress into comfy stretch-waist jeans, a white Hillborough College sweatshirt and her extra pair of dry sneakers.

In her charming room with its gabled ceiling and surprisingly feminine yellow-and-blue calico bedspread and curtains, she eyed the bed longingly. But she figured it would be best for the baby if she worked off some of the negative energy still zinging through her from her time spent with Colby.

What was it about the man, she wondered, taking her time navigating the wide lobby staircase, that one minute had her utterly fascinated and the next utterly frustrated? Just thinking about the look on his face when he'd placed his big, warm hand on her even bigger tummy to feel Baby Talbot wriggle…

Ugh. She fanned away instant tears.

This was no time to get mushy.

She was headed outside for a workout, not a blubber-fest!

Resolutely pushing her way out the lodge's front door, she stepped onto the still sunny porch—a fact that would take some getting used to, seeing how it was past nine at night. One bonus of all that sun, though, was that it was still a perfect temperature for her walk alongside the lake.

She'd just breathed in the sweet smells of fish and soaring spruce and windswept water when a clunk came from the far end of the porch.

"Colby," she said, hands to her chest. "You scared me." He sat in a rocker and had had his feet crossed at the ankles upon the porch rail, but the clunk she'd heard was his hiking boots hitting the floor. "What're you still doing here?"

He laughed. "Thinking about what I'm going to do about you."

Hands resting on her stomach, Whitney strolled his way. "I'm sorry about acting all snippy in there. You kept going on and on about us getting married, and all I wanted to do was eat, and…" She dropped her gaze, scuffed the tip of her sneaker against a raised nail on the wood plank floor.

"And?"

Did he have any idea how handsome he looked? How sexy that dimple was on his right cheek? How thick and touchable his dark hair was and how broad his shoulders were and how late at night, whenever she allowed herself to think of their time together, her insides went all quivery and weak.

She remembered skimming her hands along his chest, wondering at the strength just beneath his skin, imagining a life in which she woke up next to him every morning, secure in the knowledge that he didn't view her as a trophy or cook or chauffeur, but as a partner.

An equal in life and love.

Ha. Whitney had seen enough of her mother's and friends' awful marriages to know the only good marriage was one that had never taken place!

"And?" he prompted again.

"And, well..." She flopped her hands at her sides. "I was looking forward to us having a nice, civil conversation, that's all. While I can't foresee ever getting married, I do think it'd be best for my son if I'm at least friends with his father, don't you?"

"There you go again. Your son? Come on, Whitney, you act as if you made him all by your lonesome. Seems to me, I was there, too."

She opened her mouth to retort, but nothing escaped but a high-pitched squeak. She spun on her rubber soles, abandoning her earlier plan for a walk in favor of lounging in bed watching satellite TV.

"Oh, no," he said, broad hands singeing her shoulders as he turned her around. "Don't even think about running off on me. At least not until you admit I did most of the work in conceiving my son."

"He's my son, and what do you think I'm doing

now? Do you think lugging around this two-ton kid of yours is fun?''

"Ha!" he said. "There you go, you admitted it."

"Admitted what?" she said, trying awfully hard to slow her pulse. Colby stood close enough that his belly grazed her belly, and his warm breath fanning her lips smelled of the mint Nugget used as a garnish on his iced tea.

"That the baby's mine."

"Hello?" She rolled her eyes. "That fact has never been in contention. That's why I'm in town. To tell you my baby is yours."

"Well, then…"

"What?"

"I've had it with you," he said, releasing her to swipe his fingers through his hair. Stomping off the porch, he mumbled, "I can't imagine why I ever even slept with you. I mean, yeah, you had that almost-a-virgin sex kitten thing going—not to mention the fact that I was gonna die, but that mouth of yours is—wo-oooooh—''

Chapter Six

Colby tripped.

Not any ordinary catch-yourself stumble, but a fall of mammoth proportions all the way down the front porch stairs.

"Colby!" Whitney cried. He heard her scuttle across the porch and down the stairs. "Oh my gosh," she said, from somewhere closer to him on the gravel path. He felt one cool hand on his forehead and the other on his cheek. "Are you okay?"

He eased open his eyes.

"Thank goodness," she said with a relieved sigh. "I don't know what I would've done if something had happened to you."

Groaning, he said, "That's funny. I figured you'd be relieved to see me knocked off."

Tears shone in her eyes. "H-how could you say such a thing? Do I really come across as that heartless?"

Though every bone in Colby's body ached at that

moment, his heart ached more. He was sorry for bringing those tears to her eyes, but dammit, she hadn't exactly been playing nice.

"No," he finally said. "Here, give me a hand up, then I'm calling it quits—at least for the night. Maybe all these accidents are a sign that you're right and we shouldn't be together." Already heading toward his black Jeep, he glanced at his gravel-ravaged hands.

"You're bleeding," Whitney said, chasing after him. "Let me drive you home, then I'll bandage those up for you."

"Are you kidding? After everything you've already done, you expect me to hand you the keys to my Jeep?"

"If you do," she said with a wide smile, "I promise to at least consider your proposal. Sort of."

"Really?" he asked, raising his eyebrows.

She nodded.

He tried to reach for his keys, but she quickly caught on to his problem.

"Let me," she said, sliding her hand deep into his front pocket, setting off all manner of sparks. Luckily, once she realized his distress, she finished her task efficiently and without any cracks about him having a flashlight in his pocket.

BENEATH HIS CABIN'S soaring cathedral ceiling, Whitney dabbed Colby's fingertips and palms with a peroxide-soaked cotton ball.

They sat across from each other—Colby on the couch with his hands over a towel she'd folded on the coffee table, Whitney perched on the edge of an overstuffed armchair.

She'd expected his house to be the quintessential mountain man's digs. But while it wasn't exactly neat as a pin, the open living room with its loft, which she assumed was the master bedroom, and the roomy country kitchen made the house as welcoming as any home she'd ever seen.

Honey-hued logs rose to the polished plank ceiling, providing a suitably impressive backdrop for the river rock fireplace. She could all too easily imagine warming herself beside it on blustery winter nights….

Colby's furniture wasn't so much about style as it was about comfort. It was big and overstuffed, upholstered in a navy-and-forest-green plaid that managed to be manly yet inviting. He didn't have knickknacks gracing tabletops, just a few pictures. Most of those had been taken with a woman Whitney assumed was his mom. Other shots of him and his friends showed Colby hanging one-handed off the edges of cliffs, skiing, hamming for the camera during a skydiving free fall.

Whitney frowned, accidentally pressing harder than she'd intended on one of his deepest cuts.

Good thing Baby Talbot would be growing up a safe distance from his adrenaline-junkie father!

"Ouch," Colby said with an exaggerated wince.

"Sorry," she said, "I'm trying to be gentle, but for someone who looks like such an adventure-seeking stud in all these pictures, you squirm more than a six-year-old."

"This how you're going to treat our son?" he asked. "All gruff and businesslike without even a kiss to make him better?"

She rolled her eyes.

"Here I am in pain—light-headed and downright dizzy—and you're not healing me, you're roughing me up."

"Am not!" she protested.

"Oh yeah? Then prove you have a tender side hiding somewhere behind those soulless brown eyes."

"Soulless? Did you just call my eyes soulless?"

He grinned.

"Oh, I'll give you soulless, right in your…" What she wanted to give him was a good tongue-lashing, but thinking up a suitably insulting response would take too much energy—especially since that disgustingly handsome grin of his already had her out of breath.

Maybe a better approach would be showing him just how tender she could be?

Raising his hand to her lips, she rained hot, soft

kisses all around his wounds and right on up to the pulse points on his wrists.

He had a minor scrape on his right cheek, too, so she leaned forward, taking on the perilous task of kissing him while at the same time trying to keep her belly from grazing his.

Only she failed miserably—and on way more points than bumped bellies.

Whitney had meant her sexy ministrations to affect only him—and to prove only that she was the most tenderhearted person she knew. But when she paused, hoping Colby was ready to apologize, he was quiet and she felt strangely addled.

"How's that?" she whispered into his right ear.

He gulped. "Better. Thanks."

"Sure you don't need additional medicinal kisses?"

He shook his head.

"All right then." She eyed the latest bulge in his pocket, wishing she could forget the night when she'd grown intimately acquainted with that particular part of his anatomy. "That's, um, probably good. Now, quit whining and let me get on with my nursing."

Five minutes later, she'd applied antibiotic ointment, gauze and tape to Colby's scratches. When she placed the small square of gauze on his cheek, a twinge of guilt rippled through her. He looked so sad. If she hadn't been running off at the mouth, he wouldn't have been running down those steps to escape her.

"Can I get you anything?" she asked.

From his perch on the sofa, with his long, lean legs propped on the coffee table, he said, "There's sun tea in the fridge. Think you could pour me a glass?"

"Sure."

Heading to the kitchen gave Whitney a much-needed breather. What was it with him constantly invading her personal space?

Oh, right, like it'd been him kissing you?

There went her cheeks again.

She'd only kissed him because he'd called her soulless. What else could she have done?

Reaching into the fridge for the tea, she lingered in the blessedly cool air.

Must be some baby hormone thing turning up her thermostat. Without a crackling fire in sight, the only other thing that could be causing such unbearable heat was her frustration with Baby Talbot's father.

Right. You're frustrated, but way more because of all that time spent apart *from Colby than* with *him.*

Scowling, Whitney slammed the fridge door hard enough to rattle the pickle relish and olive jars.

Setting the jug on the green slate counter, she rummaged through various cabinets for a glass, finally finding one to the left of the sink. The sink held five dirty glasses, a cereal bowl with a few Cheerios still floating in it and another bowl wearing what she guessed to be the remains of last night's chili supper. Before she left for the night, Whitney decided she'd wash Colby's dishes for him. With his hands all cut up, he shouldn't get them wet.

She wasn't sure why she cared. Probably it went back to her generally kind nature—not that he cared about that.

She marched back across the room to the side-by-side stainless steel fridge, which had an ice and water dispenser in the door. Slipping the glass beneath the ice nozzle, she said over the mechanical tinkle and crunch, "You've got a great house."

"Thanks."

"I take it Alaskan pilots make a nice living?"

He shrugged. "I do all right. Guess I usually just go for the top of the line in most things. It's a bear getting appliances or electronics up here, let alone repaired. So I'd just as soon pay extra for quality goods, then not worry about them breaking down."

Whitney nodded. She respected his good financial sense. With luck, her son would exhibit the same sort of logic.

She poured Colby's tea, then delivered it to him.

"Aren't you having any?" he asked.

She shook her head. "After the milk incident, I'm not thirsty. I am hungry, though."

"I've got plenty of snack food in the pantry." He set his glass on the coffee table. "This time, I'll serve you."

"No," she said, pushing him back down. "You're the wounded one, remember?"

Grinning, he shook his head. "All right, Miss Independence, help yourself."

"Thank you, I will."

If he'd added a TV, Colby's pantry was so big it could've doubled as a den. A dazzling array of boxes and bags and cans contained everything from flour and canned green beans and yams to cookies and chips and—yum, more squirt cheese!

Whitney snatched a can of bacon and cheddar cheese along with a box of crackers, then headed back to the living room. "I also like your taste in snacks. Squirt cheese isn't the sort of thing I'd buy myself, but—"

"But you don't mind wolfing down mine?"

There went her stupid blazing cheeks.

"It's okay," he said. "There's plenty more where that came from. I buy in bulk."

"Gweat," she said with a happy, cheesy sigh. Mmm, squirt cheese ought to have its very own section on the food pyramid her baby books were always yapping about.

She downed another and another, having fun

making pretty patterns on the cracker tops. "What?" she asked when she caught him eyeing her. "I'm hungry."

"I see that." He grinned, and the sight of his green eyes and adorably mussed hair squeezed her heart.

Would Baby Talbot look like him?

Oh, she hoped so. God had never created a more beautiful man. Not that she was admiring Colby for her own benefit; she was merely making note of it for her son's sake.

"So," he said after a long spell of awkward silence during which all she could hear was herself chewing. "Ready for that talk on marriage?"

That brought her appetite to a screeching halt.

She swallowed her last cracker, then snapped the plastic lid on the cheese can and methodically crinkled the cracker bag shut before slipping the cardboard tab into its slot on top of the box.

"Well?" he asked again.

"I did promise to discuss it, didn't I?"

Leaning forward, resting his elbows on his knees, he nodded. "After everything that's happened today, you can see why it's imperative we get this wedding on the road. We're not much for hothouse flowers up here, but I can at least pick you a pretty forget-me-not bouquet, and Nugget'll bake us a cake. We've got a historic chapel Preach can do the ceremony in—or, for that matter, we can do it at the lodge or even right here. It doesn't matter much to me. I always figured that'd be the kind of detail better left up to my bride. Oh, you'll need a dress. I'll have to think on that one. Guess if you feel up to it, we could hop on over to Valdez or maybe down to Yakutat to buy you something lacy and white.''

''You sound as if you've got this all thought out.''

''Sure. Waiting for you back at the lodge gave me a lot of time to plan.'' And then there was the part of him that felt as though he'd been waiting his whole life to get married. To start a family. Demonstrate to his father how marriage was done. How being a great dad was done.

Colby had come damned close to sealing the deal with Margot, but with the benefit of hindsight, he figured things had worked out as they did for a reason. Margot was a Texas girl, used to the finer things in life. Looking back on it, he realized she wouldn't have lasted through the first week of an Alaskan winter. But Whitney, hell, she'd already been through the worst Alaska had to offer, and she was back for more.

''Mmm.'' She fiddled with her fingers on her lap before turning her warm brown eyes on him. ''In all that planning, did you ever think about what marriage truly means?''

He scratched his head. "I don't get the question."

Duh. Of course, he knew what marriage meant. *Forever.*

"That's my point." She sounded a little choked up. "Marriage is supposed to be a lifetime commitment, right?"

"It will be for me."

"Okay, but here's the deal. True, we shared one unforgettable night, but other than knowing we're compatible in bed, what else do we have? We're strangers. Do you really want to marry a stranger?"

He shrugged. "Don't take this personally, but this isn't so much about me wanting to marry you as it is about me *having* to marry you."

"Who says? Nugget and those nuts down at the lodge?"

"Hey," he said, raising his tea to empty it in a few refreshing swigs. "Those nuts happen to be my friends."

He stood, turning toward the kitchen for a refill.

Whitney stood, too.

"And even after taking them out of the equation, I'm going to marry you because of my son. No matter what you say, I know he'll be better off in a two-parent home." He curved his bandaged hand around her stomach, igniting a slow flame before heading to the kitchen, leaving behind those distracting waves of heat.

She chased after him, stopping beside him where he gripped the edge of the sink, staring out the window at the view that never failed to calm him. From this vantage point, a good twenty feet back and above a narrow portion of Kodiak Gorge, the jagged gray rock canyon looked impenetrable.

Hand on his shoulder, she gently turned him to face her. "Do you think your son would want to grow up in a home filled with strife?"

He felt a muscle twinge in his jaw.

"Because face it, Colby, that's what the two of us would share. Do you honestly think I'm ready just to give up my career? The life I've created for myself? If we can hardly get two words out of our mouths without bickering now, what happens when mutual resentment sets in? What kind of message would that send to a child? With me, in Chicago, Talbot will not only have love, but friends. A top-rated play group and a doting mother and nanny. The finest schools and clothes and cultural opportunities most kids only dream of. Does that sound like such a horrible life?"

He grunted. "Now, who sounds like she has it all worked out? All except for what you're going to say when *Nick* gets old enough to ask about his daddy. *Where is he?* he'll ask. *Why doesn't he love me enough to be with me?*"

Whitney crossed her arms and turned away. "I

refuse to have this discussion. The issue of Talbot's father may never even come up.''

''I wouldn't be so sure.''

''Why not? How could you possibly even know?''

''How? You wanna know how?'' He gripped her by her shoulders, dragging her perilously close. ''I damn well know how, Whitney, because I learned firsthand what it feels like to grow up without a dad. And as long as there's breath in my body, you can be damned sure I'll never bring my own son that kind of confusion and pain.''

Chapter Seven

Back at the lodge, Whitney stepped away from the window, with its spellbinding view of the sun just now setting over the lake. She should have been enchanted by the postcard-perfect scene, but all she really felt was tired and cranky. She was sick to death of trying to make that bullheaded man not only understand her point of view, but agree with it.

Backing up to the bed, she grabbed a strand of strawberry licorice before falling onto the downy comforter and pillows. She closed her eyes, sighed, chewed.

The last time she'd slept on down had been—

Okay, false start. Time to think about something else.

Anything else.

Classic TV trivia. Who would've been hotter together? Greg and Marcia from the Brady Bunch? Or the Professor and Mary Ann?

I'll tell you who was way hotter than either one of those match-ups. Colby and Whitney.

Grr. She furiously chewed the rest of her licorice.

Okay, so how many times had she been over the whole night spent in the wrecked plane? They'd both thought themselves on the brink of death. What they'd shared *ought* to have been hot. Given a choice, who wanted to die in a flurry of so-so passion?

But now, they were both very much alive.

In a way, it had been like being on vacation, when everyday stresses seem nonexistent. But they somehow always manage to reenter your life around the time you're packing to go home—to remind you that your vacation really is over.

That was how things were with her and Colby. Over.

Excitement like that couldn't last forever. It burns itself out. Kind of like her mom had burned out after all those bungled marriages. What marriage was she on now? Number seven? Or was it eight? Who could keep up?

Her most recent spouse was Neil. He owned a used car lot in Berwyn. Made a truckload of money at it, and spent every dime on his hobby of collecting railroad memorabilia. Dining-car china, silver pieces, porters' uniforms, monogrammed bed linens, signal lanterns. If it had to do with trains, he collected it. He even wore a conductor's cap to work every day, and used an old Pullman car as his office. Eight of the ten rooms in his house were dedicated to his love of trains; so was every weekend.

Whitney had nothing against trains. If anything, she found the whole era of train travel fascinating and romantic. Her problem was with the way her mother had assimilated Neil's love of trains. During their weekly mother-daughter calls, pretty much all she talked about was which new piece they'd picked up.

If it'd only been this one case, Whitney wouldn't have been worried. But with Haywood, her mom had taken up sailing. Lyle did golf. Vincent had seemed more in tune with his four dachshunds than with her mother, who, on Whitney's last visit to their happy home, had lovingly trailed after the wriggling pack, scooping up dog biscuit crumbs and a trail of shredded socks.

What was it about all of those relationships that made her mother lose herself? Or for that matter, had her mother ever been on her own long enough to even recognize who she really was?

"THERE YOU ARE, sugar biscuit," Nugget said as Whitney meandered into the lodge's crowded, sun-flooded dining room at 6:00 a.m. "I wondered what'd been keeping you."

Keeping her? Did no one around here ever sleep? "Morning, Nugget."

"Sleep well?"

Practically falling into a chair at the table beside the one she'd shared with Colby, Whitney groaned.

"I'll take that as a no," Nugget said, slipping a menu onto the table. "I'll be right back out with a nice glass of milk."

Blech. "Could you please just bring me a cup of decaf coffee?"

"I would, honey bun, but I never have understood that whole business of how they take the caffeine out of the coffee. Seems downright unnatural. Highly unsafe for the baby."

Okay. "Well, my pediatrician understands the process fairly well, and she says it's safe, as long as I don't overdo it."

Nugget shook his head. "Nope. I don't think so." He flashed Whitney a wide smile before heading for the kitchen. "Be right back with that milk."

Crossing her arms on the table, Whitney dropped her head into them and groaned.

Great. Another fun day in paradise.

"Oh good, I didn't miss you." Colby slid into the empty seat at her table, then snatched up her menu.

Whitney slowly raised her head. "Miss me? Where else would I be at this hellish hour? And where are your bandages?"

"I'm all better—see?" He held out his hands, and the gashes that had made her queasy the previous night had faded into no big deal. Maybe they *hadn't* been that big a deal to begin with—at least not in the real world.

In her mind, though…

She took a deep breath. The thought of his being hurt—no matter how small the injury—didn't sit well with her.

"And as for where else you might've been," he said, "you could've been doing just about anything. Fishing, gold panning, hiking."

"Hiking. You honestly think I look ready to hike?"

"Maybe. I know if I was a moose, I'd get a kick out of watching you waddle down the trail."

"Oh no," she said, slapping her palms onto the table. "Did you just say I waddle?"

"Darlin'," he said with a charming grin. "I've seen it—and I think it's adorable."

Talk about stealing her thunder. "Well…"

"For that matter, the head attached to that waddling body of yours isn't so bad, either."

"Um, thanks. I think."

"You're welcome. Oh, before I forget…" He eased out of his chair and knelt beside her, "Good morning in there, Nick," he said to her stomach, molding his fingers against it. "This is your dad. I just wanted to make sure you're getting an all-right start to your day.'' He shifted his hand lower, only to plant a quick kiss on the spot where his palm's heat still lingered—just in time to feel his son's response. Deep inside her, Talbot gently rolled, easing his foot in a wide arc all the way across her stomach.

Colby stared in wonder. ''Was that...?''

She nodded. For some crazy reason, tears lodged at the back of her throat.

''Well, I'll be damned...'' he said, eyes suspiciously shiny as he stumbled back into his seat. ''I mean darned. My kid already likes me.''

''He does that all the time,'' Whitney said, toying with a plastic tub of grape jelly. ''It doesn't necessarily mean anything.''

''Don't,'' Colby said, his eyes suddenly cold.

''What?''

''Deliberately set out to downplay what was for me a very big moment. Like it or not, Whitney, I am your baby's father. No matter how hard you try to reason that fact away, you can't.''

''I-I wasn't trying to.'' *All I was doing was trying to make sense out of the feeling that shot through me when you talked to our son.*

Our son.

Was that the first time she'd thought of Baby Talbot as anything other than all her own?

''I've got to make a run up to the oil site.''

''But you haven't eaten.''

His eyes brightened. "That mean you want me to stay?"

She hesitated, then said, "Ah, sure."

"Oh boy, now there was a warm welcome if I've ever heard one." Pushing his chair back from the table, he stood, pressed another quick kiss to her stomach, then sauntered out the lodge's front door.

With all eyes in the room on her, Whitney felt her cheeks flame. What? What did these people want from her? She'd done the right thing in coming up here to even tell Colby about his son. She hadn't *had* to. She could have just kept Talbot a secret, and Colby never would have known.

No, you couldn't. Not for a second could you have kept that man from knowing he had a son. It wouldn't have been right.

Lips pressed together, Whitney reached for the menu and snapped it open. Who cared what these people thought of her? It wasn't as if she was ever coming back up here again.

If those adrenaline-junkie pictures she'd seen at Colby's house were any indication of the kind of father he'd be, she was right to keep Talbot far away.

Good grief, Colby would probably celebrate their son's first birthday with a baby bungee jump off the rim of Kodiak Gorge!

"Ready to order, cupcake?" Nugget set a full glass of milk on the table.

Whitney looked up at him. "I don't suppose you've reconsidered bringing me a decaf?"

"Nope. But how about some nice eggs scrambled with ham, tomatoes and cheese?"

"I was thinking pizza sounded good. Or maybe some powdered sugar donuts."

Nugget grinned. "Ham-egg scramble it is then. I'll have it right out to you, doll."

Whitney sighed.

It was going to be a long week. Why had she chosen now to be frugal over the cost of an airline ticket?

COLBY TOOK A SEAT at one of the six round tables in Global Oil's newly decorated mess hall, then frowned. A couple of months back he remembered hauling a lot of paint over here, but yellow? Who the hell'd ever heard of painting an all-male mess hall yellow?

Of course, Dot lived there, too. But she fit in so well with the guys, no one even thought about her being a woman.

"Hey, Colby," Todd Fulmore said. The master welder set his tray on the table before easing into a seat. He winced.

"Back still giving you trouble?"

"Yeah. Though I gotta say, those new mattresses we got have made a difference—and the recliners in the game room. Heaven. That little woman you brought up here did one helluva a job in making our lives a whole lot nicer."

"You mean Whitney?" Colby took a bite of his roast beef sandwich, trying his best to look uninterested.

"Yeah, that was her name. At the time, we didn't have a clue what she was doing, but now I want her back—getting us some improvements to this food." He eyed his grayish slab of meat loaf. "Heard the two of you were an item. See her lately?"

Colby nearly choked on his latest bite. "Uh, yeah, you might say that."

"Mmm, I smell a story," Dan Dascoll said, taking another empty seat at the table. "It's been a slow week. Spill your guts."

"Yeah," Todd said. "Because, believe me, you sure don't want to hear what old Dan here's been up to."

Rolling his eyes, Colby said, "I already know. Word travels fast when it involves a five-foot-six, stacked, blue-eyed blonde."

Dan leaned back in his chair, rubbing his jaw. "Yep. Last weekend was undoubtedly one of the happiest of Heather's life."

Todd pitched his roll at Dan's wide grin, but Dan just caught it midair and took a big bite before flinging it back.

Todd made a face before shooting from three-point range into the trash.

"Out with it, Davis," Todd said. "If I have to hear about his wild nights with Heather one more time, I might just have to—"

"Take a cold shower?" Dan winked.

"All right." Colby finished off his chocolate milk. "Dan, you remember that dark-haired looker who spent a couple of months up here last winter?"

"Shoot, yeah. I made a play for her, but she was all business. Real cold, even though I heard rumors 'bout you and her gettin' real hot that night in your plane."

"Can it, Dascoll. She now happens to be the mother of my son."

In unison, Todd and Dan whistled.

"Damn," Todd said. "That was fast work. Congratulations."

"Thanks." Colby sat a little straighter. Yeah, his little guys had been pretty strong swimmers.

"So?" Dan asked. "She call you wanting child support?"

"Not exactly."

"Wait—let me guess. She wants you to get your ass down to the lower forty-eight and marry her ASAP."

Colby had to laugh at that. "I wish—except for the lower forty-eight part."

"She wants to marry you and move lock, stock and barrel into your place?"

"Since you're never gonna guess, I might as well tell you. According to her, all she came up here to do was tell me I'm gonna be a dad."

"And…" Dan stared, apparently dumbfounded.

"That's it. She just wanted to tell me, then she planned on leaving town. But I'm having none of it. There's no way in hell my son's growing up without his father."

"I can see your point, man, but she's a cool customer. One of those career women with no time for guys like us."

Nodding, Colby said, "You hit the nail on the head with that assessment."

"So? What're you gonna do?" Todd asked.

Colby shrugged. "I'd like to think there's a peaceable way out of this. Hell, I offered to marry her last night."

"But she turned you down?"

"Uh-huh."

Dan shook his head. "All I can say is good luck, man. Sounds like you're gonna need it."

COLBY HAD ALMOST FINISHED the preflight check on his plane for the return trip to Kodiak Gorge when his friend Dot sauntered up the dock. She stood about six-two, always wore her lucky red Oklahoma State hat crammed over a mess of salt-

and-pepper curls, and was renowned for the best dirty jokes in a five-hundred-mile radius. Today, though, Dot wasn't smiling.

"I heard you were up our way," she said.

"Yep, brought Pitkins a box of gaskets."

"Heard that's not all you brought."

"S'cuze me?" Colby wasn't sure he liked her tone.

"You heard me."

"Sure, but why don't you try telling me what's behind it? Something bugging you?"

"In a manner of speaking."

"Well then, spell it out." Colby stuck his head back under the cowling to check the oil.

"Okay. I heard you're gonna be a father."

"Uh-huh."

"You gonna do right by that little gal?"

"Gonna try."

"You'd better do a damned sight better 'n that."

Colby stepped out from under the cowling and wiped his hands on a rag. "We've been friends for years, Dot. I would hope in all that time you've come to know me as an honorable man."

"I *used* to think so."

Colby gritted his teeth. He'd had just about enough of being labeled the bad guy where he and Whitney were concerned.

"See, one snowy night a while back," Dot said, "I talked Whitney into knockin' back a few root beers, and she opened up like a bloomin' flower. Told me how she thought she might be pregnant, and how the only person who could be her baby's daddy was you, but how she didn't see the two of you ever gettin' much further than you already had."

"Uh-huh. And that's pretty much the way she still feels."

"You tried changing her mind?"

Colby laughed.

"You're gonna have to treat her with kid gloves. The little girl's been hurt."

"She's hardly a little girl, Dot. She's a full-grown woman with a head full of so-called progressive ideas that'd scare off a grizzly."

For the first time since his arrival, the woman cracked a smile, but far from being her usual guffaw, it was more of a wistful chuckle. "That's my girl. Got enough big-city notions to scare off a whole pack of grizzlies, but that's just it, Colby. It's all show. Inside, that girl's feelings are tangled like snagged fishing line."

Colby shrugged before pulling down the cowling and fastening it closed. "I'm real sorry to hear it, but since she's not exactly opening up to me, there's not much I can do."

Dot put her hands on her hips. "I'll tell you what you can do—*make* her marry you. 'Cause after the kind of example she's seen set by her momma, that's the only way she's gonna do it.''

"Again," Colby said, "seeing how she hasn't mentioned any family trouble to me, I fail to see that it's any of my business."

"It's your business because that baby she's carryin' is yours, and I'm assuming you want to keep that child here in God's country where he or she belongs. Am I right?"

Colby's heart pounded. "It's a boy. Her baby— *our* baby. And yes, I'd very much like to keep him in Kodiak Gorge, but his momma's stubborn. Short of kidnapping her, nothing else is gonna make her stay."

"I know. I heard all about her crazy idea of raising this baby alone. Even back before she knew for sure she was with child, the one thing she did know was that she wasn't ever gettin' married."

"She say why?"

"Her momma. Fancies herself a Liz Taylor. Been married seven times. Each time worse than the last. Our Whitney said she doesn't ever plan on ending up like that."

"Can't say as I blame her," Colby said, jaw tight as he winced at the sun shining off the lake.

Our Whitney.

A long time ago, back before their disastrous airport goodbye, he'd thought of her as his. He'd fantasized about what it might be like for the two of them to end up together. But there was a damned big difference between the vulnerable beauty she'd been that night up on the mountain and the all-business ice queen she'd been with him most of the time since.

As late as this morning, he'd held out hope of the two of them reaching an amicable agreement where their son was concerned. In other words, she'd agree to marry him on a friendly basis for now, and see where their friendship might lead.

He'd been prepared to give her one hundred percent of everything he held dear, including his heart, but she'd turned him down cold. As far as he was concerned, they'd now reached the point where the only person who could fix their dilemma was a good attorney. One who dealt with child custody situations. Because Colby no longer wanted to share their son.

He opened the plane's door. "Been nice talking to you, Dot."

"You heard me, didn't you? She's hurt. You gotta take a different approach with her type. You know, use some finesse."

"Finesse, huh?" Colby shot his old friend a broad smile. "Why don't you try that on your man, then tell me how it works?"

AFTER WATCHING Colby take off in that snazzy new ride of his, Dot picked up the control room phone and dialed a familiar number.

"Kodiak Lodge," Nugget answered.

"It's me."

"You get the job done?"

"Tried."

"That's not good enough."

"Nag, nag, nag."

"Don't you sass me. Doggone it, I'm practically that boy's daddy, and I'll not have any grandson of mine being raised in some backward town like Chicago. Probably don't have a decent steak in the entire state of Ill-noise, and who knows where a granddad can take his grandson to teach him how to properly snag a trout."

"You want me to launch Phase Two?"

Nugget sighed. "Let's give 'em one more night on their own, but if she hasn't accepted his proposal by then, it's time to pull out the big guns."

Chapter Eight

Colby rubbed his eyes to make sure that what awaited him at the end of the dock wasn't a mirage. Granted, with the tricky head wind, the flight back to Kodiak Lake had taken longer than usual, but he didn't feel tired enough to have conjured up an unbelievable sight like this.

Seated pretty as you please on top of the boulder that had forget-me-nots growing out of it, wearing jeans and a pretty pink top, was Whitney, her dark hair glinting in the late-afternoon sun.

"Hi!" she called out with a wave and smile that wiped out all his carefully made plans to tell her that if she didn't marry him, he was calling an attorney.

He couldn't do that to her.

He wasn't that kind of guy, and seeing her now, he knew she wasn't a hardball kind of girl. Just like Dot had told him, she was a softie on the inside, and it was high time he started treating her like one.

Especially since she wouldn't have come all the way out here unless she had a very good reason—like telling him she had finally agreed that marrying him was not only the right thing for their son, but for her.

Filled with a sudden calm at the notion that his whole life was about to take a welcome turn for the better, Colby took a deep breath.

Time to meet his bride.

Oh sure, technically they knew each other, but something about the sparkle in her eyes told him they were about to meet again as if for the first time.

"Hi, yourself," he said, shutting and locking the plane door before slinging his flight bag over his right shoulder. Hands in his jeans pockets, he headed for the end of the dock. "Nice day, huh?"

"Gorgeous."

"What'd you do today?"

"Bit of this, bit of that," she said, standing, then meeting him halfway. She held her hands behind her back.

"What've you got?" he asked, touched that she thought enough of him to have gotten him an apology gift. Whether she was hiding a bouquet of handpicked flowers or a candy bar from the drugstore, he'd love it. Not for the gift itself, but because she'd finally accepted the inevitable.

They were meant to be a family.

"Oh, not much," she said, still wielding that pretty grin.

God, she looked beautiful carrying his child. Complexion radiant, eyes bright. At that moment, he knew he'd never seen a more gorgeous woman.

The two of them, crazy as it seemed, were right.

"Out with it," he said. "What'd you get me?"

"Get you?" Her grin faded.

"Yeah, you know. Isn't that a gift you're hiding behind your back?"

"Um, well, I suppose you might say that."

"Oh, I get it. You want me to guess? Draw out the suspense along with the fun." He liked this new playful side to her personality. It reminded him of the woman he'd met all those months ago in his dearly departed Beaver.

"Well…"

"Let's see. Is it bigger than a bread basket?"

"Colby, I—"

"Duh. Since it fits behind your back, I'm guessing that's a no. Sorry. Stupid question. Okay, give me a second to regroup."

"Colby—"

"No, really. I'll get it this time. You brought me a—"

"Colby, would you just *listen* for a second? You and me—we're strangers. What I brought *is* a gift. A gift I had my lawyer draw up that guarantees your financial and emotional freedom from any future claim I might make on you in your capacity as my child's biological father.''

As her words—her poison—sank in, Colby's blood ran cold. At first, his heart thundered, but then it slowed to dull, furious beats. God, how could he have been such a fool? She'd played him like a damned fiddle. Sure, in a moment of anger he'd thought about suing for custody. But there was a *huge* difference between thinking about it and actually following through.

He swiped his fingers through his hair.

''Here,'' she said, holding a crisp legal-sized envelope bearing his name and address. ''At first, my attorney suggested I just mail these—to keep everything tidy. But I wanted to present them face to face. You know, make the whole thing more personal.''

Hot tears pricked Colby's eyes and he hated himself for not having seen this coming. All his life, he'd held tight to the Pollyanna image of being the perfect dad alongside his perfect wife. They'd love each other, deeply and forever. The three of them— hell, maybe even the four or five of them—would be a force to be reckoned with. Their loving bond, their *family* bond, could never be broken. But just as he'd seen how futile that dream was with Margot, he was seeing it again with Whitney. But knowing she already carried his son made the pain that much worse.

He looked at her, at the silent tears streaming down her cheeks. "Tell me," he said, swallowing with difficulty. "How the hell can you stand there so...unmoved, when I see this is hurting you as much as it is me?"

She wiped her cheeks. "Yes," she said, "it's hurting me, but not for the reasons you think."

"Oh, reasons like you're condemning our son to life without a father before he's even come out of the womb? What other reasons could there be?"

Whitney turned away—not because her decision to raise her son alone was wrong or somehow invalid, but because she couldn't stand seeing the hurt her decision had inflicted on this obviously strong, loving man.

What had she done?

Her lawyer had been right. She never should have come here—not if she expected to start her journey into motherhood with a clean conscience.

The truth of the matter was that she'd read all the books. She knew how important having a father was to a boy—but she couldn't let Colby do it. Fears that he'd pull some stunt like baby bungee jumping weren't fueling her determination to cut all ties. Truthfully, she just couldn't bring herself to make the same mistakes her mother had, over and over again.

Marriage wasn't for her. Her disaster with Rocco had been enough. She couldn't sign her life over to a man—not even a man who seemed as wonderful as Colby.

Deep inside her lurked the certain knowledge that, as far as she was concerned, if Colby turned out to be as rotten a father as her own had been, her son would be much better off never knowing him. She was saving her son years of costly therapy and pain.

"Please sign these," she said, clearing her voice. "It'll make things much easier for everyone."

He took the papers. Stared at them. A muscle ticked in his throat as his fingers slowly tightened around them.

"Colby? Did you hear me?"

"Oh, yeah," he said with a harsh laugh. "Loud and clear." He stepped closer and closer until she smelled his trademark scent of airplane and leather and sweat. He stepped nearer still, and she felt his radiated heat. And then he was there, in her personal space, daring her to flinch.

"Now, it's time for you to hear this." Never looking away from her, he ripped her papers in half, then flung them into the lake.

COLBY HAD FIGURED that after a good four or five hours, he'd feel better about the afternoon's events. But as he sat on the rough-hewn log bench tucked into the curve of Kodiak Lodge's stairs, he still felt nothing but confusion and contempt for the mother of his son. And that hurt. Granted, they hardly knew each other, but he'd been prepared to offer the woman his very heart on a silver platter. And oh, she'd taken it, all right. Taken it off the platter to shred it into a zillion tiny pieces.

And what was *he* doing?

Sitting here like a damned fool, knowing he had to yet again swallow his pride for the sake of his child.

After showing her in unambiguous terms what he wanted her to do with those papers of hers, he'd driven her back to the lodge, where she said she planned to take a nap. He'd done the same himself. When he woke up, he felt that same old familiar lead chunk where his heart used to live.

The bottom line was, he wanted his son—not just for a few weekends out of the year, but every morning. He wanted to smell his child's tiny SpongeBob jammies sticky-sweet with syrup. To feel his chubby hands twining round his neck as he carried him in from the car after he'd fallen asleep in his car seat. He wanted all the quiet times. The intimate moments part-time dads never got to see. Hell, he'd even been looking forward to sharing his son's moments with Whitney—the first time she breast-fed him or gave him a bath in the sink.

They could have shared all those special times.

Why couldn't she see that? How could she possibly think her way was best? For whom? Surely not for their son?

That was why he was back at the lodge for a last-ditch effort. He had to talk some sense into the woman. He knew she was book smart. Now was the time to see if she was common-sense smart, too. Because that was all this situation needed. Some good old-fashioned common sense.

He heard a commotion above him and stood. At the top of the stairs, Whitney—who looked twelve months' pregnant—had bumped into a side table. In the process, she'd knocked over Nugget's set of *Reader's Digest* condensed books and a few knick-knacks he kept on hand because he said they made the place more homey for his guests.

Colby had just mounted the first step to help his son's accident-prone mother, when a couple of the guys—and a gal—from Global walked in the front door.

"Hey there, Colby," Dot called out, Todd and Dan right behind her. "Long time no see, huh?"

"How'd you guys get over here?" Colby asked.

"We, um, had an unexpected cargo shipment late this afternoon. Cutty Milborn brought it in from Juneau. We, um, hitched a ride back with him."

"Okay, that explains how you got from the site down to Juneau, but what're you doing *here?* His rig can't land on this lake."

''Damn, Colby, what's with all the questions?'' Dan said. ''Can't you just be glad to see us and leave it at that?''

Head aching from his constant worrying over how to keep his son, Colby grinned. ''Sorry. Guess I'm just itchin' for a good fight.'' To show Dan there were no hard feelings, he patted him on the back before the threesome tugged him along to the lodge's bar. What the hell? What would one beer hurt? If nothing else, it would buy him a little time to compose his thoughts before his talk with Whitney....

WHITNEY HURT, and not just because that solid brass moose had fallen on her toe.

The afternoon with Colby couldn't have gone worse. She'd had the whole speech worked out in her head for months. How most men would be thrilled to be relieved of the burden of an unplanned child. And how she'd actually be doing him a big favor by agreeing to sole custody—giving him visitation rights if he wanted them, of course. The one thing she hadn't counted on was the fact that Colby would be the best father any child could ever imagine.

He didn't just want his son. He was *fighting* for his son.

And if she'd even said her next thought aloud, her friends would consider her mad. But lately, she was beginning to think she felt her son pulling toward Colby. Whenever she was around him, Baby Talbot became extra active. Kicking and rolling, arching as if reaching for his first hug.

Probably all of that could be attributed to gas, or the effects of too many fatty foods on her already thin nerves. But still, what if there *was* something to it?

She stacked the last of the books back on the table at the top of the stairs.

What if she was wrong about her son not needing a father? Even worse, what if—

"There you are," Nugget hollered from the foot of the stairs. "I was just coming to get you."

"What's up?" Whitney asked, smoothing her hair, which she'd secured in a tight chignon at the base of her neck.

"Oh, I'm just coming to wag a little fresh-baked pot roast under your always-hungry nose."

"Mashed potatoes?" Whitney asked, stomach already growling.

"Absolutely, along with plenty of gravy, a nice green salad, sugar-glazed baby carrots and, for dessert, hot apple pie."

"Mmm, I should've been down here an hour ago."

Nugget laughed. As Whitney reached the bottom step, he held out his hand to lead her into the crowded dining room.

"Aren't there any women in this town?" she asked, eyeing the all-male crowd of about twenty.

"Sure," Nugget said, bringing Whitney to her usual table beside the bank of windows overlooking the glistening lake. "But they're all home with their families."

"Oh."

"I hear you don't go for that sort of thing."

"Family? Are you kidding? My best friend back in Chicago has a huge family. I eat over there a lot. Her mom's a great cook and has so many kids, she never notices an extra person sneaking up to the table."

"Ahh, so then you do plan on settling down with a good man someday? Maybe having more little ones?"

Whitney narrowed her eyes. "If this is your way of asking if I've accepted Colby's proposal—the answer's no."

"Gracious," he said, eyes wide, hands on his barrel chest. "I wouldn't dream of asking such a personal question. That sort of thing should be left up to Colby himself. And speaking of that dear boy… Look, here he comes. Hey, Colby! Over here!"

Whitney skimmed the faces in the small male mob to see only one.

Even though all Alaskan men seemed to grow taller and more muscular than others, her baby's father was in a class all his own. Even with his dark hair ruffled and a shadow of growth on his cheeks, his green eyes were mesmerizing. The look he cast her way filled her with shame for the cavalier way she'd handed him those forms.

He'd deserved better. At the very least, a heck of a lot more tact.

"What a nice surprise," Nugget said, patting Colby's back.

That easy camaraderie sparked a curious bolt of envy in her. She didn't realize how much she missed simple human closeness.

Waking up after having made love, she'd found the air in the plane painfully cold, yet inside their cozy down nest, Colby's naked skin had burned against hers. How well she remembered turning to him while he still slept, feeling free to touch him, outlining the silhouette of his shoulders and chest in the darkness, pressing close to drop kisses on his whiskered cheek, loving the sharp sensation of stubble against her lips.

Her leisurely exploration had awakened him, and he'd drawn her into his arms, growling like a lovable old bear as he'd playfully rolled on top of her. He'd supported just enough of his weight so she didn't feel crushed, yet he'd rested on her in a way that let her know he was all man. He'd sheltered her, yet at the same time—

"Care to call a truce?" Colby said, drawing out the extra chair at her table.

"Sure," she said, flashing him what felt like a wobbly grin.

"Can I bring you both the pot roast?" Nugget asked.

"Sounds good to me," he said, raising heat in her cheeks with his concentrated stare. "Whitney?"

"P-please," she said, somehow having forgotten just how appealing Colby could be when he tried. Or was he always this appealing, and she'd just been so focused on keeping him out of her life that she'd forgotten how much fun life could be with him?

Stop it, she told herself. Thoughts like these had landed her mother in seven failed marriages.

Nugget made his way back to the kitchen, stopping to shake hands and slap backs at each table along the way.

It didn't matter that the two of them were surrounded by people; suddenly Whitney felt as if they were, once again, alone.

"I like your dress," Colby said.

"Thanks." She glanced down at the simple blue-and-white cotton toile dress with its empire cut. It was her favorite of all her maternity clothes—the one item she still felt pretty in, despite her ever-growing girth. "Colby?"

"Uh-huh?"

"I'm sorry."

"Me, too. I shouldn't have thrown your papers away like that."

"No. I mean, yes. Yes, you should have. I mean, we're both adults here, and even though I can't see myself ever getting married, I didn't mean to come across like some baby-making robot."

He shrugged.

She gave him a halfhearted smile. "I'll take that to mean I was as callous as I feared."

"Well…" He took her hands and gave them a gentle squeeze.

Warmth eased through her, and when the baby kicked, she gasped at the intensity.

"You okay?" he asked.

"Yeah. Our, uh, little slugger here must be ready for dinner. He's raising quite a fuss."

"Do you mind?" he asked, releasing her hand to reach across the small table.

Assuming he meant to curve his fingers and palm to her big belly, she guided his hand, then covered it with her own.

Baby Talbot rolled, and Colby's eyes lit up. "I think he likes me."

"Much as I hate to say it, I think you're right."

"You don't have to make it sound like such torture."

"Sorry," she said. "Again. It seems like all I've done since I got here is apologize."

"And I feel like that's my fault."

"No. Not at all. Here I'm supposed to be trained in helping people improve their lives, yet my own life is a mess."

"I wouldn't go that far. You've been blessed with my baby, haven't you?"

"My, aren't you the modest one."

He winked, and her resolve to close her heart against the memories of the magic they'd shared melted a bit more.

After dinner, when Nugget automatically brought Colby a coffee, Colby politely declined in favor of a glass of milk.

"You didn't have to do that, you know."

"Sure I did." He forked up the last of his hot apple pie. "What you're going through—it has to be tough. You need to know you're not alone."

What she would've given to hear those words during her first trimester. The mornings she'd been sick. The nights she'd lain awake confused, wondering if she could handle being a single mom. Knowing sadly that in light of what she'd learned about marriage, she had no other choice.

You're not alone.

It was a lovely sentiment, but aside from her son, she *was* alone, and always would be. For the fleeting moment she glanced up, only to lose herself in

Colby's luminous gaze, the knowledge causing her a pang of sadness.

Then she reminded herself that loving someone hurt. She'd given love a try with Rocco, and look where that had led.

No, she was smart to stick to her resolve. It was one thing to be lonely. It was totally another to be consumed by soul-crushing pain no amount of aspirin could ease.

At a loss for words, Whitney looked down at her pie.

It had been much easier to convince herself that she was doing the right thing back when Colby had been so obstinate. This charming side, the side she'd first been attracted to when he'd shared his grape Bubble Yum, was a definite drawback.

"What's your favorite movie?" Colby asked.

Pleased by the lighter tone of their conversation, Whitney sighed. "I don't know. You go first. There are so many, I'll need a second to think."

"Okay. Let's see… On any movie list, *Terminator* and *Independence Day* would have to be high, along with *Alien* and *Aliens,* but the last two in that series?" He shook his head and grinned. "Your turn."

"I'm still thinking. I've spent so much time studying, and then working, I haven't seen that many movies. You go again. It's fun hearing what you like."

"Hmm, to show I'm not all action and do have a sensitive side, *Last of the Dogmen* and *Sleepless in Seattle.*"

"Whoa. Even I've seen that one, and it's definitely not your average shoot 'em up action flick."

He shrugged. "What can I say? I'm a well-rounded guy, fully qualified to make a great dad and husband."

"Colby," she warned. "This has been such a nice night. Please don't start."

"I'm not starting anything—just putting in a plug. You know, like a five-second campaign speech." The little-boy grin he shot her way somersaulted over her every objection, sending her pulse racing and her attraction meter spiking.

What was she going to do if her son had the same ability to melt her heart with just one glance? How was she going to spend the next eighteen years separating him from his father, when every look reminded her of the man she was trying to avoid?

"You all right over there?"

She looked up, straight into his worried eyes. "I'm fine."

"You sure?"

Swallowing hard, she nodded. Oh, why had she ever come here? Colby was a good man who'd make a great dad, and maybe he'd even make someone a great husband—just not her. "I think I'm ready to call it a night."

"Sure," he said, standing to help her out of her chair. They'd long since paid the bill. Or rather, he'd paid the bill, even though she'd insisted Nugget charge their meal to her room. "Sorry. I should've noticed you were getting tired."

"I'm a big girl, Colby. Please stop acting like my well-being is your responsibility."

His large hand deliciously warming the small of her back, they walked out of the considerably less crowded room. Only two other tables were occupied, by sportsman types wearing outfits fresh off the pages of an L.L.Bean catalogue.

In the shadowy cove of the stairs, he paused to take her hands in his. "Look, Whitney, what you just said, about not being my responsibility? You've got that all wrong."

The warmth in his eyes made her mouth feel dry.

"You see, from the moment you first climbed on board my plane, you *became* my responsibility. Your life was quite literally in my hands."

"Yes, but in case you haven't noticed, we've landed safely."

"Have we, Whitney?" He drew her closer, easing her hands behind her back, fitting their bodies together like two puzzle pieces. She licked her lips. "Look at me," he said.

Helpless to do anything else, she did.

"Do you think for one second that anything about this situation is safe? For god's sake, Whitney, we're talking about a baby. My baby—yours. You act as if this is some kind of game you're determined to win, but it's so much more. A whole life is at stake, and—"

"Sixty-seven bottles of beer on the wall, sixty-seven bottles of…"

Colby groaned. Through the lodge's front door tottered ten or so very drunk Global Oil guys with Dot and Dan at the helm. Brody, Tanner and Sergei followed close behind.

"There's our man," slurred Dan. "And look, he's got his bride-to-be with him, too."

"Excellent," Tanner said.

From out of the dining room stepped Nugget, along with Henry, Stanley, and all three cooks and dishwashers.

"What's going on?" Colby asked as the crowd came closer. He slipped his arm around Whitney.

"What do you think is going on?" Dot asked.

"I-I'll just be heading on up to bed," Whitney said with a funny little giggle as the crowd of at least twelve or thirteen men and her friend Dot surrounded them. At least ten more people streamed in from the bar.

"Sorry, sugar bun," Nugget said, "but this here is an Alaskan intervention, and you'll be going nowhere but where we send you."

"Oh, no," Colby said. "You're not really going to—argh!"

Too late for protests, he and Whitney had already been hefted off their feet and propelled toward the door.

Chapter Nine

"Let me out of here!" Whitney shouted, banging on the delivery truck's metal door. Outside, a lock clicked into place.

"Good job, boys," Nugget said, his voice muffled but chipper. "Dot? Brody? You two grab the coffee I packed for the ride, along with that milk for our expectant momma?"

"Yessir."

"Let me out!" Whitney screamed. "Are you people *nuts?* This is kidnapping! *Double* kidnapping!"

Colby, drawing Whitney onto one of the comfy pillows lining the truck's floor, said, "Wouldn't that be a triple kidnapping, or don't I count?"

"Grr," she said, eyes flashing in the oddly romantic light of at least fifty green glow sticks. "Tell them to stop, Colby. This isn't funny."

"Hey," he said, holding up his hands in surrender. "You see me laughing? I'm just as much a

victim here as you. And look on the bright side."
He pointed to a heart-shaped basket filled with a
bottle of sparkling cider, crackers and Whitney's
favorite squirt cheese. "At least they gave us
snacks."

She made a good show of frowning, but couldn't
quite hide the twinkle in her eyes when her gaze
landed on the cheese.

The truck engine started. From outside, Nugget
hollered, "Don't you two worry about a thing.
Brody and Dot were just pretending to be drunk.
They're both sober as preachers on Judgment Day.
They'll get you where you're going, nice and
safe."

Colby groaned, spotting boxes of what he
guessed were supplies in a corner.

"Okay, hit it!" On Nugget's command, the truck
lurched forward, flinging Whitney against Colby's
chest.

He shook his head. "Sometimes I wonder if all
the isolation up here isn't throwing a few people
off their rockers."

"This thought just now occurred to you?" Whitney asked. "Aggh!" A tooth-jarring pothole left
her holding on to Colby for dear life.

"Hey!" Colby shouted toward the truck's cab.
"You two fruitcakes mind slowing down?"

They did, and thankfully, although the ride was
still bumpy, the bumps became easier to bear.

A few minutes later, Whitney realized she was still clinging to Colby, her arms around his neck, her cheek pressed against the warmth of his chest. She knew she should let go, but didn't want to. He was not only a safe harbor in this bizarre storm, but a comfortable one.

"We're gonna be all right, you know," he said, stroking her hair. She nodded against him. "This is what my so-called friends consider an Alaska-sized therapy session."

"Yeah, but where are they taking us, and what do they hope to achieve?"

She felt him shrug. "Probably some cabin out in the woods. Most of us have places out in the boonies we use to just get away."

At that, she leaned back and cast him a grin. "Oh—like the stress of being around all two hundred or so occupants of this town can be a strain?"

"Hey, try over a thousand occupants. Kodiak Gorge is a happening place."

"Sorry."

"You should be." He tweaked her ear.

"What was that for?"

"Sass. Now, where was I?"

"Explaining why your high-stress lifestyle requires you to get away."

Shaking his head, he said, "You're incorrigible."

She laughed.

"Anyway, I imagine they're planning to leave us wherever they drop us off until we either bicker each other to death or agree to marry."

"They have to know we can't be manipulated like that."

Back to stroking her hair, he said, "Oh, I don't know. When Nugget gets a hankering to do something, there's no stopping him. He did this to my friend Tanner and his wife Jenny when they announced they were getting a divorce."

"So? What happened? Are the two of them still married?"

Sighing, Colby said, "Guess they fell under the category of bickering each other to death. I have to confess to being in on that kidnapping, though. After their time together, they never spoke to each other again."

"Wow."

"Yeah. That's kind of how I felt."

On that note, Colby cradled Whitney closer, glad when the steady rise and fall of her breathing told him she was asleep.

There weren't many roads leading out of Kodiak Gorge. Two, to be specific—Old Gold Road and New Gold Road. And Old Gold Road should've been downgraded to Old Gold Mule Trail about twenty years back. Judging by the increase in bumps, Colby guessed they were on the trail.

The one that led straight to his fishing cabin.

Dammit, he knew Nugget and the rest of the gang meant well, but having Whitney in his town was hard enough. Why in the world would they believe he wanted her up at his sanctuary? Especially since every time he cast out his fly rod from now on, he'd be thinking of what quiet joy could be found in having his towheaded son standing right there beside him, proudly holding up his first fish.

The strange thing about that image was the absence of little-boy-Nick's mother. Did the fact that Colby couldn't imagine her in his future mean he was destined to only see his son part-time?

No. The very idea was unacceptable. He snuggled his son's mother close, settling in for a long, bumpy ride—both emotionally and physically.

"WHITNEY, HON, wake up." Colby eased her from his chest, grinning at the tiny wet spot in the middle of his dark green shirt where she'd drooled sometime in the night.

"No," she said, snuggling closer. "It's too early."

Moving her off him and onto one of the dozens of pillows lining the truck's floor, he tried the door, and it slid right open. Hand to his forehead, shielding his eyes from the blinding sun, he was treated to the sight of one of his favorite places on earth— his log fishing cabin in all its rustic glory, nestled among towering Sitka spruce, mountain hemlock and cedar.

Between the trees the lake glittered.

As far as Colby knew, the lake didn't have a formal name. He'd always just thought of it as his lake. Although now, oddly enough, he was looking forward to sharing it with Whitney.

Usually, he flew in, and the aerial view of his private paradise always filled him with quiet pride, but the place was just as sweet from this angle. Even though Whitney was a big-city girl, he couldn't imagine her not forming an instant attachment.

Turning to her, he knelt, sweeping her thick hair back from her ear so he could whisper, "Wake up, sleeping beauty. We're home."

Still lying beside her from when she'd needed a late-night snack was a can of squirt cheese. Knowing she'd be wanting another hit soon, he put it in his pocket for later.

"Yoo hoo…sleeping beauty. Time to rise."

She swatted at him. "I already told you it's too early to wake up."

"Mmm," he said. "Judging by his momma, our son's gonna be a bear to wake up for school every morning."

"He'll go to night school," she said, eyes still closed, a grin tugging the corners of her mouth.

"That's all well and good," he said, taking her

hands in the hopes of making her sit up. "But last I heard, Kodiak Gorge didn't offer late-night kindergarten."

"They would for our boy—he'll be special."

Colby's spirit soared. "That mean you've rethought your plan to head back to Chicago?"

Her eyes popped open, and she bolted upright. "What?"

"What you just said—you know, about our son being special, and how Kodiak Gorge would open a kindergarten just for him. That mean you're sticking around?"

"No—absolutely not. I was half-asleep. I wasn't in my right mind after not getting a moment's decent rest."

"That's funny," he said with a wry laugh. "Most of the night, your snoring kept me up."

"I can't help it," she said, scrambling to her feet. "All this dry air up here messes with my sinuses."

"Oh."

"It does."

He hopped down from the truck, then held out his arms to help her.

"Thanks," she said, "but I can do it myself."

"By all means," he said, stepping aside. "I wouldn't dream of interfering."

"Thank you."

Using the side of the truck for support, Whitney

started to jump down, but the truck floor looked to be a good two feet off the ground, so she opted for another approach, figuring she'd squat, turn around, then hop down backward.

But considering how her belly got in the way, that wasn't working, either.

"Need help?" the know-it-all standing beside her inquired, laughter in his tone.

"No," she muttered from between clenched teeth.

"Sorry. Just asking."

"Yeah, well, don't."

She next tried a forward squat, but when she felt queasy, she turned around again, thinking it was just a matter of—"Oooh!"

Colby snatched her from behind, briefly cradling her before setting her on her feet.

"I said I could do it," she barked.

"You're welcome."

Hands on her hips, she glared at him. But facing that handsome, warm-eyed mug of his, all whisker-stubbled and kissable like it had been on that snowy night, she couldn't hold onto her anger—especially since she would have had to resort to asking for his help eventually. "I'm sorry," she said. "I do appreciate your assistance."

He shrugged. "It wasn't a big deal."

"It would've been in about five minutes if I hadn't got to a bathroom." She grinned. Hand to her forehead, she looked around, then said, "This place is straight off the pages of a storybook." A few seconds later, she added with a wince, "A nice, happy storybook, if you'd kindly show me to the facilities."

"Sure. Right there," he said, pointing to a crude path leading off into the trees.

"What? Is this cabin like a storage shed, and the real house is down that trail?"

"No, I just mean the bathroom is down the trail."

"Oh—like you've got a bathhouse," she said, already on her way. "That's cool. A bubble bath would feel fantastic."

"Just keep walking," he said. "I want it to be a surprise."

She flashed him a smile. "Mmm… Maybe this whole kidnapping thing won't be so bad after all. Kind of like a spa weekend."

"Just keep walking," he said. "You can't miss it."

With a perky wave, she rounded a bend in the path. Leaning against the truck, arms folded, Colby crossed his legs at the ankles, then counted. "Five…four…three…two—"

"An outhouse! Your only bathroom is an outhouse?"

Dot and Brody came charging up the other path that led to the lake.

"What's the commotion?" Brody asked. "There a grizzly?"

Colby let out a snort. "Oh, there's a grizzly, all right. A big old momma grizzly who just found out there's no flush toilet."

"That's my cue to beat it," Dot said, hopping into the back of the truck to grab a box Colby presumed held supplies. "Brody, help me out. I want to be gone before she comes back."

"For crying out loud," Colby said. "You're not really planning on leaving us here, are you?"

"If we don't," Brody said, "Nugget told us he wouldn't serve us for the next year."

"And you two actually believe that?"

Brody had already dumped one box onto the dirt at Colby's feet and was going for another.

"Aw, don't leave me up here with her. She scares me."

"Yeah, well you shoulda thought about that before you—"

"Speed it up, Brode—this here's the last one." Dot hefted the last box off the truck, yanked the back door down and secured it, then hightailed it around to the cab.

Brody followed hot on her heels.

Colby wasn't far behind them. "Come on, guys," he wheedled. "You know how well this worked with Tanner and Jenny, so what in the hell makes you think it would work with—"

They'd shut and locked both cab doors.

Dot started the engine, grinding it into first gear.

"Hey!" Colby pounded on Dot's door, chasing the truck out of the cabin's yard. The place used to have a driveway, but since he'd never used it, sometime over the years it had blended with the forest—a fact made only too evident when a birch sapling whipped his left cheek. "Ouch. Dammit."

In the time it took him to mutter a few more curses, his two supposed friends and their truck vanished behind a dust cloud.

Raking his fingers through his hair, Colby muttered, "Behold, the power of Nugget's home cooking on a bachelor and an old married woman who between them can't open a can of soup."

"Where's the truck?" Whitney asked, eyes wide. "All the squirt cheese was back there—and those yummy little crackers with the—"

"Do you like trout?"

"What do you mean?" she said, eyes narrowed, hands on what was left of her hips. "They just went off for a quick bite to eat at a restaurant down the road, right? After that, they'll be back in a couple of hours?"

He sighed.

"Colby? They will be back, right?"

"In a few days."

AFTER WHITNEY GOT OVER the initial shock of realizing she wasn't going anywhere, Colby planted her on a comfy rocker on the cabin's screened porch, then hauled in the supplies. There were lots of them, including her suitcase and toiletries from the hotel.

She'd offered to help, but he still seemed under the impression that just because she was pregnant, she was also helpless. Normally, she'd have delighted in proving him wrong, but—she yawned—this was one time when she was happy to abide by his macho request that she rest.

Granted, the outhouse thing was a real drag. And instead of a proper stove, the kitchen had a wood-burning monstrosity that looked as though it had been hauled up here in gold rush days. But sitting as she was now, gazing out at the view, she was surprised that she couldn't think of anything she'd rather be doing—and that included working at the job she loved.

The control freak in her should have been railing. Instead, Whitney felt an odd sense of peace. If pressed, she couldn't have even explained why. For whatever reason, this cabin was where she needed to be.

The diamond-shot lake was ringed by spruce. At the far end stood aspen in a field of wildflowers. Behind those was a snowcapped mountain. In the patch of enchanted forest serving as a yard, a wood-pecker had his way with a half-dead cedar, and from over the lake came the occasional honking of geese.

The sweet smell of wood smoke hung in the air. Colby must've gotten the stove to work. He'd explained earlier that he couldn't light a fire in the rock fireplace because a bird family had moved in for the summer.

"You cold?" Colby asked, strolling through the cabin's open door with a fuzzy red blanket.

"Maybe a little," she said, cuddling into it when he tucked it over her lap. "Thanks."

"You're welcome." He pressed a tender kiss on her forehead before heading back inside.

The baby kicked. "Colby?" she called out.

"Yeah?"

"Despite our differences, let's try to have a nice time up here—for however long those so-called friends of yours decide to leave us."

"Sounds good to me. Anything you need?"

"Other than that bath I was wishing for, along with a snack, I'm pretty much content."

"You really want a bath?"

"It'd be nice, but I'm guessing that the only shower or tub up here is the lake, right?"

He winked. "What do you want for a snack?"

"Colby? What? Do we not even get the lake to bathe in? Is it infested with ultra-hardy piranha or flesh-eating arctic bacteria?"

"Snack?"

"Pizza?"

"How about baby carrots and ranch dip?"

"Yum."

Yet again avoiding her hygiene question, he disappeared inside the cabin.

Wrapping the blanket around her shoulders, she followed him, only to be pleasantly surprised by what he'd done with the place in the past thirty minutes. On her first trip through, the sofa and few chairs had been shrouded in old muslin dustcovers, as had the bed, giving the whole cabin the appearance of ghost central.

But now...

Now it was a cozy haven with a gently worn red sofa and chairs, and a big wrought-iron bed, fluffy and inviting with its mounds of pillows and cheery, red-plaid spread. Above the rock fireplace hung an uncannily accurate watercolor rendition of the lake.

Colby caught her appraising the room and reddened.

"What's wrong?" she asked, admiring the red-calico curtains with their pretty lace trim.

"What's wrong?" he asked with a slight cough. "I'd forgotten how girly this place is. My mom painted that," he said, pointing to the picture Whitney had just admired. With any luck, their son would inherit her artistic flair. "I used to spend so much time up here that she redecorated the place for my twenty-fifth birthday. Guess she thought I could use it for a love nest.''

Now it was Whitney's turn to redden. "Well?"

"What?"

"Did you? Use it as a—you know.''

He looked sharply away.

For a second, Whitney couldn't figure out what would make Colby react that way, but then understanding dawned. As much as she wanted to believe he'd never been with any woman but her, she wasn't that naive. "You came up here with Margot, didn't you?"

He nodded.

"And knowing how well that turned out, you're figuring the same is about to happen with me.''

"Actually,'' he said with a half laugh, "I was thinking more along the lines that at least with Margot I'd had a fighting chance, but with you…''

"Oh—you think I should agree to give up my entire life—my work and friends? Just because you want me to?''

"No, because our son needs you to. He's a kid. Can you imagine what a kick he'd get out of coming up here? Fishing, camping, learning how trappers and miners used to live off the land.''

"Getting bitten by mosquitoes,'' she said, slapping at a little sucker about to tear into her arm.

"God help him if he's even half as bullheaded as you.''

"Why am I bullheaded just because I know what I want?"

"Because you're so caught up in knowing what you want, you can't even see what our child needs."

Chapter Ten

Whitney should've been enjoying herself.

Here she sat in a steaming copper tub, complete with berry-scented bubbles. Not only that, but perched pretty as you please on a table beside her was a tray of snacks—the squirt cheese she'd feared long gone in the truck, and those little round crackers she'd come to adore. Sweet grapes and slightly tart apple slices. Best of all, a tall glass of sweet herbal iced tea Colby had cooled by sticking the whole plastic jug of it in the frigid lake.

Cheese cracker in one hand, tea in another, the rest of her immersed in sinfully warm water, she should've been content. But from just outside the window came the sharp whack and ker-thunk of Colby splitting logs in two, then the halves hitting the ground.

From the moment they'd stepped out of the truck that morning, he'd been working while she lounged. Never in her life had she felt so useless—

unless it came to making her mother listen to objections concerning her latest marriage.

Her mother's experience had shown her what an all-around disaster marriage would be. Cooking, cleaning, watching nothing but sports on TV. Always having to put your needs below someone else's. Of course, Whitney would do all of that and more when Baby Talbot came into the world, but until then—no siree, Bob. She wasn't about to go turning her life upside-down for some man she hardly knew.

Oh no—of course not. Especially when it's so much easier just sitting around on your tush letting him do all the work for you.

Whitney squeezed her eyes shut. From outside came another thwack and ker-thunk, then whistling. It was cheerful whistling, even though he still had to have a few painful places left over from his fall down Kodiak Lodge's front stairs.

"Baby," she said, curving her hands around her belly. "Your father's a workaholic, and your mom's turning into a whine-a-holic."

Her only answer was the occasional plip-plop coming from the old-fashioned hand pump beside the sink.

Colby was a good man. Judging by what her single friends said, a really good man was an increasingly tough breed to find in this day and age. He was handsome and loyal and honorable and hardworking. And here she was grousing about how she'd never marry anyone, let alone a man like him, when he was working so hard to make her time at the rustic cabin enjoyable.

Okay, so she'd established the fact that she was behaving like a spoiled brat, but what was she going to do about it? There was no way he'd let her help cut wood.

Maybe there were other things she could do? She could cook or dust or pick berries, or whatever else mountain women did to help their men keep food on the table.

Not that Colby was *her* man.

Scrambling out of the tub, Whitney hastily dried herself on the fluffy white towel Colby had been thoughtful enough to provide, then dressed in black warm-up pants, a white T-shirt, and the matching warm-up jacket. After adding thick white socks and comfy shoes, then securing her ponytail, she headed outside. To her surprise, Colby wasn't at the neatly stacked woodpile where she'd thought he'd be.

"Colby!" she shouted, swallowing a twinge of panic. What would she do if he'd been eaten by a bear or had fallen down some rotted old mine shaft?

"Over here!"

With relief, she spotted him at the lake's edge, fluidly casting a fly rod in and out. He'd changed into a navy-blue T-shirt, and with each cast, the muscles of his shoulders and back flexed. Remembering only too well the feel of those muscles beneath the sensitive skin of her palms, Whitney licked her lips.

Carefully making her way down the dirt path, she called, "Catch anything?" *Besides my heart?*

"One. But I figured since you probably want to eat, too, I might need to catch a few more."

"A *few* more?"

"Hey, it's not your fault that kid of mine is always hungry."

Having reached him on the shore, she reached up to tweak his ear.

"Hi." He sent her a quick grin before once again casting out. "I thought you were relaxing in the tub?"

"I was," she said, plopping her behind on a smooth-topped boulder, wincing when the cold seeped through the thin fabric of her pants. "But then I got thinking about how hard you've been working ever since we climbed out of that truck, and I started feeling guilty."

"Aw, this isn't work," he said with another cast and another grin. "This is as close to heaven as I figure I'm gonna get on this earth."

"You like fishing, huh?"

"Yep, always have."

"When did you learn?"

He shrugged. "Seems like I've always known. But I guess, looking back on it, I used to tag along with my friend Brody and his dad. He was a pretty cool guy—half Athabascan Indian. Died of a sudden heart attack a few years back." Colby threw out another cast. "Anyway, he taught us to tie our own flies, and he was a real stickler for not catching more than we could eat. We must've fished every river and lake round here for a couple hundred miles."

"Wow, I'm impressed. Sounds like I'm angling with a pro."

His expression took on a wistful glow. "I'll never forget my first big catch—a forty-pound king salmon. Man, did he fight. Toward the end, I was beginning to wonder if that sucker was bigger than me. Brody's dad put it on ice for me till we got home, so I could show it to Mom. I wanted to save it, but we didn't have the money to take it to a taxidermist, so Mom thought she'd try tanning it by scooping out the insides, then hanging it on the clothesline." Still wearing that far-off expression, he chuckled. "After it dried, she moved it to the shed to try making it into a pillow or something, but whatever she'd done didn't work, and the thing started stinking. One morning I went out to the shed before school to look at it, only to find the shed door had been busted in, and a black bear was munching my poor fish for breakfast."

"Oh, no!" Whitney said, hand to her mouth to hide her horrified smile. "What did you do?"

Grimacing while throwing another cast, he said, "Truth? Flat-out bawled. Mom let me stay home from school sick."

"She sounds sweet."

"Uh-huh."

"She still happy with her new husband?"

"Uh-huh."

"Please tell me if I'm overstepping the bounds here, but you told me your dad left the two of you. How old were you?"

"Six. He took off the day before my birthday. Mom and Nugget held this great party for me down at the lodge. All the town kids came. My friends Brody and Tanner. Streamers, balloons, cake. But through the whole thing, I stood at one of the lodge windows, just waiting for my dad to get there."

"How awful."

"Yeah, well, crap happens."

"But you were just a little boy. Did he leave a note, or at least call, or what?"

"None of the above. One day I thought we had this perfect little family. The next, he was gone."

"Wow. I'm sorry." Whitney swallowed hard, thinking back to the day her father had left. There'd been nothing mysterious about it. Thanks to the volume of her parents' fights, she'd known he was moving in with his secretary, then filing for di-

vorce. From that time on, he'd sporadically taken
Whitney on trips to the Brookfield Zoo. He probably figured he'd done the best he could by her,
but somehow it'd never been enough. She'd wanted
so much more. His opinions on her art projects.
Time watching a TV show together. The chance to
play the cakewalk game together at school carni-
vals.

Sometimes she'd wished he'd vanish.

She'd always thought it would've been easier
never having known him at all than knowing he
was out there, living just a few miles down the
road. So close, and yet far too busy to waste his
time on her.

And now here was Colby's story of his own
messed-up father, which proved that even if her dad
had just disappeared, it wouldn't have been any
easier.

So how did that affect her convictions about raising her son without a father? It left her more confused than ever.

"Don't be sorry, Whitney. I'm over it. And anyway, it's not like it's your fault."

"I know, but—oh, look! You caught one!"
Whitney's animated cry echoed all the way across
the lake.

"Come here," he said, edging toward her with
the pole. "Reel him in."

"Oh, no—you do it."

"Really," he said, one arm around her shoulders urging her to her feet, flooding her with warm awareness of his size. "It's high time you learned how to catch your supper."

She stood and he put his arms around her, awkwardly shuffling the rod into her hands. His hands cupped hers, making sure she held the rod tight and away from her stomach.

"Okay," he said, "start reeling."

She did. When her tingling fingers slipped, he was there to catch the reel, starting her again. "Pull back," he urged.

Laughing and breathless, she did.

On the lake's sparkling surface, the trout leapt, landing with an impressive splash. "Look at him!" she said. "He's huge!"

Laughing along with her, Colby said, "I'd offer to make him into a pillow for you, but..."

"That's okay, but thanks for the thought."

Tugging hard on the rod, he said, "You bet."

They stood there together, reeling in the fish, for what felt like the longest time, when it had probably only been minutes. He was still fighting as Colby unhooked him, then added him to an antique basket.

"That was fun," Whitney said once he'd rinsed his hands and was again standing beside her.

"I'm glad you enjoyed it. I wasn't sure."

"What do you mean?" she asked, shading her eyes from the sun.

"Just that, you being a city girl and all, I thought you probably wouldn't get a kick out of something as mundane as fishing."

"Nothing about that was remotely mundane," she said, helping him gather his pliers and a khaki-colored vest covered in more fishing flies. "Though I have to admit that this is the closest I've come to hunting up my own dinner—unless you count picking a lobster out of a tank."

"Nope." He carried the rod and basket of fish in one hand, resting his free hand on the small of her back.

Not only did his touch warm her, but it made her feel safe and secure, as if she was someone to be looked after and cherished.

It was a lovely feeling and quite unexpected.

Soon, she thought, she'd have an entire new life to care for, in the form of a child, at least for the next eighteen or so years. But then what? She wasn't about to saddle her son with one of those needy mothers who expected him to dedicate his life to her. What happened after he left the nest? What happened when she was once again on her own with nothing to warm her but memories of perfect days like this?

"You're awfully quiet," Colby said, slipping his

trout rod into a hollow log holder on the cabin's porch.

"Mmm…just thinking."

"About the baby?"

She nodded. "How did you guess?"

"When you think about him, you have this funny protective way of holding your stomach."

Lips curved upward as she followed him to the small fish-cleaning station at the porch's far end, she said, "I've never noticed, but I guess you're right." She looked down to find herself doing it again and laughed. "Oops."

"Don't sweat it. It's cute." Scaling her fish, he added, "Besides, I like knowing you're already watching out for the little guy—even if you do hit the squirt cheese a bit too hard."

Leaning against the porch rail, she grimaced. "Guilty as charged. Need any help?"

"Nah. Why don't you go on inside and take a nap? I'll wake you when lunch is done."

"Colby, I'm not an invalid."

"Did I say you were?"

"No, but…"

"You've already put in a full day lugging my kid around."

"Are you for real?" she asked with a shake of her head.

"What do you mean?"

"I mean, you're flawless. You're like some textbook example of the perfect guy. Don't you ever loaf around doing nothing? Or burp real loud, or leave your clothes all over the floor?''

''Sorry to disappoint you, but what good would any of that do?''

''I don't know, I just…'' She tugged her sweat suit zipper up and down. ''Part of me feels like you're too good to be true. There's got to be something about you that's bad.''

''Why?''

''I don't know. Just because.''

''Let me guess,'' he said, filleting the bones out of the fish. ''If I'm not some womanizing chauvinistic creep, you don't have a convenient out.''

''Excuse me?''

''You heard me. If I'm a bad guy, then you're the good guy by default. You're not only right in keeping me away from my son, but you're noble. You're taking the high road, while I'm a few thousand miles away where you can forget all about me. Then you can tell our son anything you want. But you wanna know something, Whitney?''

Swallowing hard, she raised her chin.

''Whatever you say to him, you're going to know the truth. Whatever you decide at the end of the week, you're gonna know I *am* a good guy. I'd be a caring, considerate husband to you, and a damned good father for our son. So hey, if you decide at the end of this week that none of it matters and that you'd be better off sailing this family ship all on your own—well, you can just take that up with my lawyer. But in the meantime, I want you to know what you're passing up.''

''Are you done?'' she asked, swiping tears from her cheeks with the backs of her hands.

''Not hardly.''

''Great. Then I guess I'll take you up on that offer of a nap.'' Turning her back on him and his speech, Whitney stormed into the cabin and threw herself on the bed.

Chapter Eleven

"Smooth move there, bud," Colby mumbled under his breath a good twenty minutes later as he eased a blanket over Whitney's sleeping form, tucking the fringed edges around her toes. He'd wanted to chase after her right away, but since he'd been covered in fish guts, it had felt all wrong.

Why had he spouted off at her like that?

After getting over the initial shock of being kidnapped, he'd actually sent up a silent thanks to his friends. They'd realized that all it'd take to convince Whitney that both she and their son would be happy up here was a few days alone in the true Alaska. Once she saw the majesty of the land surrounding the cabin, not to mention what an excellent provider he could be without a supermarket, she'd have no choice but to concede that he was right—the two of them should get hitched. As for her job, he wasn't all that clear on exactly what she did. But if she'd worked here once, why couldn't she do it again?

Could it really be that simple? Suddenly he wasn't so sure.

Here he'd been working his butt off for her, yet nothing he did seemed good enough. And he was starting to get the feeling that nothing he'd ever do would be good enough. Particularly since she'd already made up her mind to leave.

With a resolute sigh, he headed into the kitchen to stoke the fire in the old woodstove.

Cooking was always a challenge up here, but the food tasted so much better that it was worth the extra effort—extra effort he was now doubly determined to make in the hope of making Whitney forget their latest argument.

As he melted pats of the butter Nugget had packed, then added chopped garlic cloves and the trout fillets, Colby's mind wandered to the time he and Whitney had met.

Their first night had been so...incredible.

How had everything else gone so wrong? What was he missing?

He tossed a box of ready-made pilaf into butter simmering in another pan, then sliced off the rough ends of a bunch of pencil-thin asparagus.

This last run he'd made to Global, Dot had let him have it. Telling him he'd better treat Whitney with kid gloves. She'd rambled on about what a rough childhood Whitney had had, and how that mother of hers had set such a rotten example.

Stirring the pilaf, then adding water, it occurred to Colby that a part of him was tired of the fight. Tired of always being the one making concessions.

But then he remembered the ultimate prize.

A son.

How long had he dreamed of becoming a father? Forever.

And if he was even half the man he'd professed to be out on that porch, then no matter how many times he had to suck up to Li'l Miss Independence, he'd do it. This wasn't just about him, but also about his son.

"THIS IS DELICIOUS," Whitney said, swallowing her last bite of trout before sipping lake-chilled sparkling cider. "Thank you."

Across the candlelit table, their glances met, and she hastily looked down. What had happened out on the porch still felt too real. Too raw.

"You're welcome. Any ideas as to what you want to do tomorrow?"

"What're my options?"

He forked up a bite of fish. "Since we've already established that hiking is out, I've got a boat. We could row around the lake."

"That'd be nice."

"Good."

"Good."

Whitney bit her lip hard as tears welled up.

She hated this…this feeling of stiff formality between them.

Worst of all, he'd been right.

Every word he'd said out on that porch was true, but that didn't make any of it easier to bear. Okay, so he was the one guy in a million who might make a great dad or husband. That didn't mean she could simply blink and forget all the painful memories of her own absentee dad, or the disasters her mom and assorted divorced friends had made of their lives.

Yes, it would be so easy to believe that if she gave marriage a chance, her life might turn out differently than her mother's or her friends'. But what if she was wrong? It wouldn't be just her own life she was messing up, but her son's. From where she stood, she didn't think taking that kind of risk was an honorable thing to do.

"*E.T.,*" she said a few minutes later, sick of the silence.

"What?"

"*E.T.* You asked me the other night what my favorite movie was. That's it. *E.T.* I cry every time I see it."

He sighed, obviously as fed up with their awkwardness as she was. "What do you want to do, Whitney? 'Cause we can't keep fighting. It isn't good for you or the baby."

"I know," she said, bowing her head, hating the fact that yet again he was right.

"Don't look away from me," he said, reaching across the small table to tuck his fingers beneath her chin.

"Why not?"

"Because you're beautiful. I want to see you."

She glanced up with a faint smile. "How come, no matter how determined I am to distance myself from you, I feel like we keep getting closer?"

With a shrug, he said, "I'm guessing it has something to do with my cooking."

Tears still clinging to her lashes, she sniffed before laughing. "You're probably right."

"Of course I'm right. I'm damned good-looking, too. Our kid's probably going to be the next Brad Pitt."

"You think?"

"Oh heck, yeah."

They shared an impromptu toast of cider.

"*The Parent Trap*—both versions," she said. "I'm a sucker for anything Disney."

He glanced over his shoulder as if checking to see whether anyone else was listening. "Me, too. But what kind of man admits to getting a kick out of kid flicks?"

A good man. An even better father.

"That damned *Pocahontas*. I was baby-sitting a couple of Brody's nieces, and the first thing they did was pop in that flick. I swear, by the end, they'd run off outside to play football, and there I was sitting in the living room bawling my eyes out.''

"Quit," Whitney said, laughing so hard that she was tearing up all over again. "You're going to make me pee."

"Oh? And that's a bad thing? Like my bathroom accommodations are lacking?"

"They're lacking, all right—lacking a flush toilet!"

"That's it," he said, shoving back his chair to storm over to her side of the table. "Now you've done it."

"Colby! What—agh!" He hefted her into his arms, heading out the back door. "What are you doing?" she asked, breathless from laughing.

"You said you had to pee, didn't you?"

"Yeah, but in a real bathroom."

"Oh—so now my sweet little outhouse isn't even real? Would you prefer going behind a nice, tall spruce tree just like the bears?"

"No, I…" He'd carried her midway down the outhouse trail. With her arms wrapped around his neck, her lips inches from his, she was aware of him as she hadn't been since all those months ago, when they'd been forced together in a cramped cockpit. He was hard yet soft, and he smelled of butter and garlic and trout.

Before she could stop herself, her fingers had

wandered to the back of his head, easing into his coarse hair, urging him to press his lips to hers.

Leaning against a tree, he settled her deep in his arms, groaning as she opened her mouth, searching for his tongue. This was lunacy, yet she felt powerless to stop. This undeniable attraction had brought them together. Now, with his baby growing inside her, part of her wanted him back.

She kept telling herself they were strangers, but that now seemed a lie. At this moment, she knew him as intimately as her next breath.

"Whoa," he said, pulling away, breathing hard. "What're you doing, Whitney?"

"I don't know," she said, resting her forehead against his chin. "Does it matter?"

"Heck, yeah, it matters. I can't just turn all of this on and off. Not now. With the baby, it goes much deeper than sex between us."

"I know."

"Do you?" he asked, setting her on her feet, forcing her gaze to his.

She wrenched her chin from his hold, throwing her arms around him in a hug—not a sensual hug, but a confused one.

"Talk to me," he said, hugging her fiercely in return. "Tell me what you're thinking."

"I don't know," she said against his chest. "That's the problem. Just when I think I'm doing the right thing by heading back to Chicago, something reminds me of that night—of the way you made me feel. Safe. Like as long as you held me in your arms, nothing could ever go wrong."

If you became our son's full-time father, would he feel protected, too?

"I'm glad I made you feel that way, Whitney, but it's nothing I can sustain. Something in life always goes wrong. I can't prevent that. I'm just a man. All I can promise is that whatever rough patch we hit, we'll get through it together."

She nodded.

"Still have to go to the bathroom?"

"Yeah."

He reached for her hand, interlocking their fingers. "Come on, I'll walk you the rest of the way."

LATER, BACK INSIDE, Whitney asked, "How long does it take to get used to the fact that it's always daytime?"

"Don't know. I've never known the sun to do anything but what it does here." Colby glanced up from his task of putting fresh-smelling sheets and a blanket on the sofa. Whitney had changed into pink silk pajamas.

"We're both adults," she said, slipping a red flannel pillowcase onto his pillow. "We could share the bed without incident."

"You so sure about that?" He winked.

She reddened, plumping his pillow before dropping it at the end of the sofa.

"Come on, then, let's get you settled in for the night."

"I can put myself to bed, you know."

"Uh-huh." He pulled back the red down comforter, and she climbed in between navy-blue sheets. Once she'd settled her head on the pile of pillows, her dark hair fanning around her, he tugged the covers back, tucking them tight around her toes.

"You're spoiling me."

"Uh-huh. Good night," he said to her belly.

"Good night."

He blew out the three candles that had been lighting the room, but even with the shades drawn, at a few minutes past eleven, it wasn't completely dark.

"Brr," he said, climbing into his own makeshift bed. "Sorry about there not being a fire."

"It's okay. It's not like we could evict the bird babies."

"True."

Whitney pulled the covers up to her neck. "Thanks for a nice night."

"You're welcome."

"And next time we play checkers, I'm beating you."

He laughed. "Dream on."

Funny that he'd use the word *dream.* Aside from

their one war of words, the rest of the day had been as perfect as a dream. Catching the fish. Sharing Colby's delicious meal. The mock battle on the way to the outhouse that had ended in an epic kiss. Warm and funny conversation over three games of checkers.

Throughout the day, she'd drawn contrasts between him and her mother's men. Whitney had complained that her mother had constantly bent over backward to serve her husbands, but with Colby, the case was completely opposite. As much as Whitney had wanted to help out, he wouldn't let her, claiming she needed to rest.

Without him she would've been lost in this wilderness setting, but with him, she felt happy and secure.

Trouble was, none of this was real. It was a vacation. In a few days, their kidnappers would return them to Kodiak Gorge.

In a couple of months, Baby Talbot would be born, and she'd no longer be so clumsy and vulnerable. There'd be no need for Colby to watch out for her. Doubtless that was when his true colors would show.

"Tell me a story," she said, for her child and for herself. She wanted to collect memories of the way Colby was now, instead of the way he'd inevitably turn out to be.

"'Bout what?"

"Surprise me," she said, her voice reaching out to him in the eerie almost-dark.

"When I was a kid, my mom worked hellacious hours at the lodge. It wasn't that she wanted to, but I guess she had to. After school, she used to haul me back down there, and I'd get bored. I resented her for not just letting me stay home alone."

"How old were you?"

"Nine. Ten. Somewhere in there. Brody's mom ran the grocery store, so she was never home, either, but Brody got a choice of either staying on his own, or going out with his dad on welding jobs. Mom said I was all she had left, so she needed to keep me close."

He rolled over and sighed.

"I knew she was doing her best," he went on, "but I remember this feeling of suffocation. Like I had to get away."

"But you were so young," Whitney said, rolling onto her side to face his voice, resting her cheek on steepled hands.

"Yeah, but once my dad left, I matured fast. Mom tried being brave, but I used to hear her crying in the middle of the night. I'd go into her room, you know, just to tell her everything was gonna be okay, and she'd grab hold of me, squeezing so hard sometimes I thought I was gonna break. I wanted to help her, but I couldn't."

"What'd you do?"

"Ran away. Nugget took me and Brody and some other guys up here on a camping trip once. It used to be an old fur trader's cabin, but over the years it got run down, and pretty much anyone who wanted to use it did. I'm still not sure how she did it—maybe through the state *Homestead Act*—but Mom gave it to me for my eighteenth birthday."

"Okay, but wait. You were nine or ten, and just ran away up here?"

"Uh-huh."

"But it's so far! How long were you gone? Your mom must've freaked."

"I left her a note."

Panic welling in her throat over what she'd do if her son ever tried such a stunt, Whitney said, "So I'm assuming some sort of rescue crew came out for you the next day?"

"Nah," he chuckled. "In the note, I'd told her where I was going. She already knew Nugget had taught me how to live off the land."

"And…"

"And she climbed into the family Jeep, brought me all my schoolwork for the week, then told me she'd check back on Saturday."

"And you were nine?"

"Maybe ten."

"Wow."

"What?"

"She sounds like an incredible woman."

"She is. I'd like you to meet her one of these days."

Slipping out from under her covers, Whitney winced when her feet hit the cold hardwood floor. Then she hustled over to the couch to give Colby a big hug.

"What was that for?" he asked, yanking off the back sofa cushion, then tugging her down beside him, drawing the covers over them both.

"I feel sorry for you."

"Why?"

"I don't know. You were just a little boy. I wish you'd never been put in the position of feeling you had to run away."

"Oh, I don't know. I think it was probably good for me and Mom. I got my space, and she learned to trust me and rely on herself."

"Still…"

"What?" he asked, pushing strands of her hair over her shoulder.

"You were just a baby."

He laughed. "I was a baby the day before my sixth birthday. By the day after, I'd been forced to grow up."

"Oh, Colby." She hugged him again, only this time, her heart went out not only to him, but also to her unborn son. What was she doing, dooming him to a childhood like Colby's, without a dad? But on the other hand, hadn't he just pointed out that after a few growing pains, he'd essentially been fine?

She kissed him on his whisker-stubbled cheek, then said, "If you could snap your fingers and bring your dad home, would you?"

"No."

"That was fast."

"It's the truth. From the second I realized the bastard wasn't coming back, I didn't care. It was like a light switch flicked off inside me where my feelings for him were concerned."

Whitney's training had taught her it couldn't have been that simple. "There had to be more to it than that," she murmured.

"Nope."

"Oh, come on," she said, wishing the room were brighter so she could see his expression. "Weren't you scared? I mean, didn't your mom try looking for your dad? You know, thinking he could've been hurt?"

"Can we please change the subject?"

"Sure, but—"

He silenced her by moving his hands to her cheeks, then kissing her. Hard at first. Urgently. Then softly, making her limbs sluggish and weak.

He shifted, wrapping his hand around her belly. She angled into him, overcome with emotions raised by his kiss and by having him so close to their son.

As intensely as she'd tried pretending this baby was solely hers, she could no longer do that. This man, this soon-to-be father, was real—and growing more so by the moment, as he flooded her mind and body with memories of the night they'd made this miracle growing inside her.

"Take me back," she said.

"Where?"

"To that night. The way things first were between us."

"Why?" he asked, his voice hot in her ear.

"Because it was good. Fun."

She edged up, reached under his shirt, pulling it off. She wanted his bare skin against hers.

She wanted to feel safe, the way only he had ever made her feel. Even if it was just for one more night or, if she was lucky, the rest of her brief time in Alaska.

Crying now, for reasons she couldn't begin to fathom, she dragged her own shirt off. "Just make love to me. Make me feel like you did that night."

"Whitney, no," he said, his breath warm and moist on her collarbone where he'd just pressed an openmouthed kiss. "You don't know what you're saying."

"Yes," she whispered, raining kisses down his chest. "Yes, I do."

Hands gripping her shoulders, he pushed her back. "Then tell me why."

"Because I..." She bowed her head.

"I'd like to flatter myself by assuming it's because you love me, but since you keep refusing to marry me, I'm guessing that's not it."

Silence.

"And, sure, maybe it's just because you're hot for me, but since the woman I know isn't the type for casual sex, that's not it, either."

Silence.

"Bringing me to the granddaddy reason of them all. You feel guilty about your plan to leave here with my son—but somehow, I don't even think that's what this is about. I think it's deeper, even more selfish than that. I think you want to have raw, mindless sex with me because, just like that night up on the mountain, it'll make you forget. That night, you wanted to forget the fact that you very well could've died." He shook his head. "So let's hear it, Whitney. What're you trying to forget tonight?"

"That was uncalled for," she said softly.

"But you don't deny it's the truth?"

Escaping to the bed, she muttered, "Can we please just get some sleep?"

"Sure, Whitney. Let's sleep. But if you think you're going to wake up in the morning with this whole thing behind us...you're wrong."

Chapter Twelve

Long after Colby's soft snoring told Whitney he'd fallen asleep, she lay awake, cursing him yet again for being right.

What was he doing? Reading her mind?

Yes, she had been trying to forget.

Trying to forget she'd ever met Colby Davis.

Meeting him had been akin to catching a most pleasant virus, one she hadn't been able to wipe from her system. He was noble and caring and funny and a good listener and cook. And now she was carrying his son. And he wanted to marry her, but she couldn't marry him because she refused to give herself up. She refused to abandon her career.

And that was her right.

She didn't have to marry her baby's father if she didn't want to.

The only problem was, the more time she spent with Colby, the more she feared that maybe, just maybe, there was a part of her that did want to marry him.

What did that mean?

She'd only been back in his arms for a couple of days now, yet she felt as though they'd never been apart. With a few well-aimed verbal arrows, he had the uncanny knack of slicing straight through her every charade. Yet his words, however naked they left her feeling, were meant to be thought-provoking rather than cruel.

After this last go-round on the sofa, he'd actually shifted out from under her, then scooped her into his arms to carry her to bed. After tucking her in, he'd placed a tender kiss on her forehead, then quietly whispered good-night.

Why didn't he ever thunder and rage? Why was he always such a gentleman? Why did he always have to be the perfect embodiment of the kind of man she'd dreamt her son's father would be? Why couldn't he be rude or overbearing or obnoxious?

If I'm a bad guy, then you're the good guy by default. You're not only right in keeping me away from my son, but you're noble. You're taking the high road while I'm a convenient few thousand miles away where you can forget all about me.

Was that what she wanted? To forget him?

Did she never want to see his easy smile again? Or remember the way he smelled of sun and sweat and airplanes? Did she want her son growing up in the city, or learning to live off the land like his dad had done at such a tender age?

When Whitney was ten, she'd spent a lot of time worrying about her mom, but she'd also played with Barbie dolls and friends. She'd have had no more thought of running away than of flying to the moon.

For all her grousing about how tough it had been when her folks split, she'd still managed to have a pretty normal childhood, all things considered. Colby, on the other hand, felt he'd become a man at the age of six.

Maybe that was why she was so devastatingly attracted to him? Because he was truly a man in every sense of the word? He provided not only for her physical needs, but her mental ones. She was tired. And a part of her selfishly wanted someone else to help her with life's daily grind.

But then maybe, in its purest sense, that's what marriage truly was? A melding of emotions and lives and responsibilities that, if done right, would indeed be a wonderful thing? But countless case studies—as well as her own mother—proved that making marriage a partnership instead of a dictatorship was a near impossible task.

Armed with that knowledge, why would Whitney even want to try?

Maybe because being married to a great guy like Colby just might be worth the effort?

DETERMINED TO GIVE her brain, fogged by all these questions, a much-deserved day off, Whitney woke bright and early the next morning vowing that today she'd show Mr. Perfect a thing or two about cooking—namely, that she was every bit as good as he was.

Although to see him now, one leg hiked over the sofa back, one leg on the floor, covers askew, snoring loud enough to wake a hibernating bear, one would doubt he was a master of back-country cuisine.

Not wanting to wake him, she straightened his covers, covering his poor cold toes on the floor.

After struggling to dress herself in a fresh jogging suit, then jogging on out to the so-called bathroom, she stood in front of the kitchen stove, wondering what to do next.

Having been a big fan of the *Little House on the Prairie* books and TV show when she was a kid, Whitney knew the first step was starting a fire in the beast's belly.

Colby, being the efficiency guru that he was, already had a galvanized aluminum bucket standing by with twigs she assumed he used for kindling. Also readily available were extra-long kitchen matches and small logs.

Okay, so all the necessary equipment was there. Now all she had to do was make a fire.

Ha! Famous last words.

Thirty minutes later, she had a fire all right—a raging inferno that had turned her sunny-side-up eggs into charcoal briquettes!

Coughing and blinded by smoke, Whitney reached for the cast-iron frying pan, but forgot to use a pot holder and jumped back in pain. By the time she'd grabbed one of the oven mitts hanging from a rack on the wall, the toast she'd thought was browning burst into flame.

"Colby!"

In seconds, he came running to her aid. "What the—"

"Help! My breakfast is on fire!"

"I see that," he said, calmly reaching beside the stove for a fire extinguisher, then putting out her meal. That done, he opened the window and used a cookie sheet to fan the smoke. "You should get out of here," he said. "It can't be good for you or the baby to be breathing all this smoke."

"But, Colby, I—"

"Out," he said, hands over her shoulders as he marched her out of the room. "Ugh, it's smoky in the living room, too. Okay, time for a new plan."

"What?"

He snatched his blanket off the sofa, wrapped her in it, then gave her a gentle push toward the paned door leading out to the screened porch. "Go. I'll bring you some tea."

"But I wanted to cook breakfast for you this morning."

"How about you settle for eating a good breakfast for me?"

"Ha ha."

He pressed a sweet kiss to her forehead, then opened the door and nudged her outside.

Whitney huffed her way into a comfy chair, put her feet up on the porch rail and glared at the breathtaking view.

Brilliant blue sky, sparkling blue water, woodpecker at it again, yadda, yadda, yadda.

The place was gorgeous.

She got it.

What she also got was that never in her whole life had she felt like such a klutz.

How was it that for twenty-six years she'd managed to take care of herself just fine—better than fine, judging by her last raise—yet out in the woods she couldn't survive ten minutes on her own? Talk about an ego blow.

Even worse was the fact that, not fifteen minutes later, the resident mountain man carried out a tray loaded with two plates of steaming hotcakes and sausage!

"Mmm, that smells good," she said, unable to fathom how he'd managed to prepare the feast in such a short time. "Where'd you get the meat?"

"Nugget packed a bunch of perishables on dry ice."

"Nugget's good," Whitney said through her first sinfully delicious bite. "You are, too. This tastes decadent. I'm talking major caloric sin."

"Thank you—and yep."

"Is there nothing you *can't* do?"

"What can I say? Unless a guy wants to be at Nugget's mercy for food, he's gotta learn to fend for himself."

"Or find a wife."

"Nah." He winked. "In my case anyway, I figured why should I burden myself with a wife when I can already do everything for myself?"

"Everything except bearing a son?" The syrupy taste in her mouth turned sour. Here, all along, she'd been under the assumption that like the men who'd married her mother, Colby would expect her to conform to his every wish and command. Maybe he truly did want just her son. Once he legally had him, Colby wouldn't care whether she stayed or left.

"That was a joke," he said, nothing the least bit funny about his tone. "You know that, don't you?"

She nodded. Of course she knew he'd been joking. What was wrong with her? She was starting to sound out of her mind. Colby was a wonderful man—of that she was sure. He wanted his son near him because, even though the baby wasn't even born yet, he already possessed a deep love for the boy. As for marrying Colby, it was the best solution for sharing their son.

Whitney knew the solution was logical, but how could she know it was right?

"Aw, man," he said, setting his plate on the porch rail, then taking hers to do the same. "I wasn't going to let on I knew this, Whitney, but when I was up at Global the other day, Dot—"

"No. Don't tell me she told you about my mom."

He nodded. "Look, I can see where watching your parent go through so many failed marriages would be enough to scare anyone off. But you've gotta understand that if we were to do this thing— get hitched—" He went down on his knees in front of her chair, clasping her hands. "I'd want to do it right. And I'm not just talking about the ceremony, but the life. I don't want a forced marriage, but a real one. I'm not looking for a housekeeper or nanny for my son, but a companion. A best friend. Not someone I can share chores with, but someone I could *love*."

Giving his big, warm hands a squeeze, Whitney dared to raise her gaze to his, and what she saw took her breath away.

Beyond his rugged good looks was a burning intensity telling her that not only did he fully intend to fight for what was his, but that he also intended to win.

She dared to ask, "That woman you just described. That friend you want to call a wife. You think you might've found her in me?"

When he bit his lower lip and looked away, her heart sank. Of course he didn't love her. He'd only said that with time, he *could*.

"If you don't love me," she said, her voice small against the breeze whispering through the spruce, "why do you keep asking me to marry you?"

"Because it's the right thing to do."

Holding on to him for dear life, she asked, "But just because something is morally right in the eyes of society, how do you know it's right in here? Where it counts?" Releasing him, she pressed her palms to her chest.

He shrugged, molded his hands to her stomach. "For whatever reason, Fate brought us together all those months ago. And now, because of the life we've created, we might be meant to come together again. I guess there are some things you just have to take on faith."

Faith.

Now there was something she hadn't had in a while—if ever.

If she were raising her son alone, faith could come in handy. Faith in a lot of things. Faith in his teachers to do a good job. Faith in his friends not to lead him astray. Faith in him to always do the right thing.

Raising her son alone.

The thought was daunting. But after Whitney's father had left, her mother had refused to do anything on her own, even raise her child. That had led her straight into seven unhappy marriages.

"I DON'T KNOW about this, Colby. Are you sure it's safe to hike right up to them?" She cast a worried glance over her shoulder, not seeing that she was close to tripping over an exposed root.

"Of course," he said, guiding her past the obstacle, then shooing a mosquito from her back. "And this isn't really a hike, but a scenic stroll." Colby took her hand, slowing her down so he could watch where she was going as their footsteps fell silent on the thick layer of spongy spruce needles.

This trail with its pungent conifer smell and tunnel feel had long been one of his favorites. Sun slanted at lazy angles through the trees' enormous branches, spotlighting giant ferns at their feet. As a kid, it'd been easy to imagine himself roaming among dinosaurs in this place. This far inland, it was a natural oddity, and as an adult, he'd learned to appreciate how special it truly was.

"Believe me," he said, "once we get there, you won't be sorry. I've been watching bear families here since I was a little kid, and I'm still alive to tell the tale, aren't I?''

''Yeah, but I read on the flight up that, statistically, people are more likely to be killed by a bear in Alaska than by a taxi in New York City.''

He stopped her in the middle of the trail to kneel in front of her belly bulge. ''Did you hear that?'' he said to his son. ''You're not even out of there yet, and already she's trying to squash our fun.''

''Hey, someone has to be the grown-up here.''

''And who was the grown-up this morning who set the toast on fire?''

''Oops.'' She shot him a sheepish grin. ''That was different.''

''Right. Meaning, if you mess up, all is forgiven, but if I do—''

''Whoa,'' she said, palms flat against his chest. ''Does that mean you're admitting you messed up by bringing me here? 'Cause if so, I'll be happy to get back in the rowboat. All that rowing was nice and peaceful, but—''

He put his fingers to his lips. ''Shhh. Look.''

A good twenty yards off the trail, in a grassy clearing, a momma black bear fished for dinner from a gurgling stream, while her two cubs frolicked in tall grasses.

''Listen to their little growls,'' Whitney whispered, eyes wide and shimmering. ''Oh—and look at their mom, turning back to give them a scolding look.''

Guiding Whitney a few yards further down the trail, he gestured for her to sit on the rough-hewn log bench he'd constructed when he'd been a teen. ''Black bears rarely stray more than five miles from where they were born, so I probably watched that momma play when she was a cub.''

Whitney wrapped her arms around Colby in a hug.

''What was that for?'' he asked.

''For bringing me here. At first I thought this was crazy. I mean, who actually goes looking for bears? But this was exciting—way better than seeing them in a zoo. Thanks. You were right. It was definitely worth the walk.''

''So all I get for hauling your behind up here to see a spectacle that most city girls only see at the zoo is a measly hug?''

''Well…''

The size of her smile toppled his heart, making the thought of her returning to Chicago in just a few short days incomprehensible. She and baby Nick had to stay here. They just had to. His son needed to see bear cubs play every summer weekend. He needed to know this trail as well as he knew the route to school. And to know that rose hips were delicious, but baneberries—like the ones within reach from this bench—were poison.

"I suppose just this once I could part with more—assuming, that is, that when we get back to the cabin you'll start dinner."

"We just had lunch."

"Yeah, like an hour ago."

He fished a granola bar from his jacket pocket. "Here. Don't say I never gave you anything."

"Likewise," she said, planting her hands on his clean-shaven cheeks for a kiss.

Sweetly, she pressed her lips to his, coaxing his mouth open with her naughty tongue, slipping her inquisitive fingers around his neck and up into his hair.

When she groaned, he hefted her onto his lap, his hand pressing her closer.

Why couldn't she see that here, now, what they shared was human perfection? Life just didn't get any better than this, especially with their son between them.

When she eventually pulled back, breathless and dazed, they looked up to see the momma bear frozen midstream watching them, ears perked. A few seconds later, she gathered her troops, chasing them into thick woods.

"Oops," Colby said, tucking flyaway strands of Whitney's long, dark hair behind her ears. "Guess she only wants her cubs watching G-rated tourists."

"Hey," she said, swatting his chest. "Who are

you calling a tourist? I've got half a local growing in here.'' She patted the baby.

Feeling high on entirely too much fresh air and sunshine and kisses, Colby tossed out, ''You know, it wouldn't be too hard to make you a local, too.''

''I know.''

''Does that mean you're at least thinking about staying?''

The tremulous look she cast his way gave him cause to hope. ''Raising our son among all this would be nice, wouldn't it?''

The mere thought had Colby swallowing tears. Since his emotions had swelled to the point that he feared he'd be unable to speak, he nodded.

''Hey,'' she said, brushing back the hair from his forehead. ''You okay?''

''Um, sure. Heck, yeah.''

''I don't believe you.''

''Okay, then, I guess I'll come right out and say it. I want my son to have all of this as his back-yard—not just as his once-a-year, week-long vacation.''

''I don't blame you,'' she said. ''This place, it's gorgeous, but—''

''Wait. If I'm going to be one hundred percent truthful with you, Whitney, you've gotta know that I want you here, too. There's so much I want to share with both of you.''

"Oh, Colby…" She raised her hand to his cheek, and he leaned into her touch.

"I'm not even sure how it happened, but I'm getting to like you—a lot. I want to be with you. All the time. You've become like…a pet I want constantly by my side."

"Gee, thanks…I think."

"God," he said, smacking himself on the forehead. "That came out all wrong. I didn't mean that you were like a dog or cat, I meant—"

She put her fingers to his lips. "Shh. When I was a girl, I had a Yorkie. His name was Samson, and he went everywhere with me. He was my very best friend, and to this day, sometimes when I'm lonely or confused, I wish I had him around. You know, as an impartial ear to bounce off my nuttier thoughts and ideas." She took a deep breath, wiping at a few stray tears with the backs of her hands. "Jeez, what is it about you, always making me cry?"

"I don't know, but I guess if a guy told me I looked like a dog, I wouldn't be all that happy." He grinned, and she kissed him again.

"I loved Samson—a lot," she said, close enough for him to feel the heat of her words on his lips. "So when you compare me to a favorite pet, believe me, far from taking it as an insult, I took it in the true spirit in which I suspect you meant it— as a high compliment. Thanks."

He kissed the tip of her nose. "You're welcome."

Taking her hands, he helped her off his lap and onto her feet. Once he'd stood, as well, he took her right hand in his, then led her back down the trail.

"You like spaghetti?" he asked once they were almost back to the boat.

"Sure. Why?"

"Nugget put Italian sausage in our supply pack, along with a big tub of red gunk I'm guessing is his famous sauce."

"Yum."

"I'll even let you cook the pasta."

She glanced over her shoulder to stick out her tongue.

They'd walked a little while longer in companionable silence when she said, "Um, Colby…"

"Yeah?"

"Remember when you showed me how to tie that knot for the boat?"

"Yeah?" His stomach sank as he saw sun flash off the rowboat's aluminum hull.

The hull that, instead of resting on shore as it had been earlier, was now bobbing merrily in the dead center of the lake.

A stiff breeze had come up since they'd left, and the once glassy lake was now dotted with whitecaps. Just beyond Frazier's Peak, the snowcapped mountain in front of the cabin, storm clouds loomed.

"Sorry," Whitney said, nibbling her lower lip. "Looks like I might need another knot-tying lesson."

Lightning cracked and thunder rumbled in agreement.

Colby just stayed silent.

Chapter Thirteen

"Do you think the boat will ever come back?"
Whitney asked from the comfy rocker that Colby
had placed in front of the kitchen stove. Blessed
heat radiated from the ugly beast, leading her to
suspect that if it continued playing nice, they might
one day be friends.

"Eventually," he said, stirring the fragrant sauce
that had her hungry stomach growling. Shooting
her a wink, he said, "Don't sweat it. It's not that
big a lake. I'll hike around in the morning to get it
once it washes ashore."

Outside, thunder rolled as rain pummeled the
cabin's tin roof.

"The lake sure felt big, hiking around it in this
storm."

He shrugged. "I've been caught in worse jams—
like, say, that time we crashed our plane into a
mountain. Ring any bells?"

Twirling a lock of her still-damp hair, she made a face.

"You look awfully comfortable over there. I thought you were making the pasta?"

"I was, but then you starting poking fun at me, so now I figure I'll just sit here and watch you make the pasta."

Already at the sink filling a large pan with water from the well, he said, "I can see it now. If we do end up hitched, I'll spend the rest of my days at your beck and call."

"Only if you want more babies," she said, tucking her red blanket around her still-nippy toes.

"Do you?" he asked, putting the pot of water on to boil, then pulling out a chair at the small table.

"I don't know. I've been so busy with work, I guess I've never much thought about it. I mean, I always wanted at least one child, but I guess, yeah, it might be fun for Baby Talbot to have a little brother or sister to play with."

He winced. "Could you please stop doing that?"

"What?"

"Calling *my* son Baby Talbot. His name is Nick."

"I hate to rain on your parade there, fella, but—" Judging by the stern set of his lips and jaw that he was no longer teasing, Whitney said, "I'm sorry. I can see that helping pick our baby's name might be important to you.''

''You think?'' He sprang to his feet, then crossed the kitchen and began furiously stirring the sauce.

Whitney pushed herself up from her chair, letting the blanket fall to the floor.

At the stove, she stepped behind Colby, sliding her arms around his waist, resting her head between his shoulder blades. With their baby nestled between them, if it weren't for the rigid set of Colby's back, all would have been right with the world.

''I'm sorry,'' she said, giving him a squeeze. ''Nick it is. It is cute, in light of the night he was conceived. And anyway…it's the least I can do.'' After all, Colby probably wouldn't be seeing his son for a long time. The very thought made her always-healthy appetite fade.

How was she going to do it? Just walk away?

What she'd felt for her dog Samson was nothing compared to what she feared she was beginning to feel for this intriguing man.

Still, no matter how much she'd come to enjoy Colby's company over the past few days, she had to remember that their bond was only temporary. Her own mother had proven that the percentage of marriages that were real was minuscule compared to the ones destined to end in divorce. And what about her friends in college who'd married only to quickly get a divorce? And those were just the people she knew. How about all of those bickering couples on *Dr. Phil?*

Whitney didn't want her son going through the kind of pain she had when her folks broke up. Shoot, for that matter, Colby himself had suffered the same fate, and he hadn't thought it was any more fun than she had.

And look what had happened between her and Rocco. Now, there was a full-on relationship disaster!

Shielding their son from future pain was the right thing to do.

The responsible thing.

The *only* thing.

Turning to face her, Colby kissed her hard, making her mind and heart spin. "Marry me," he said. "And not because of the baby, but because of what the two of us share."

"I can't," she said.

"Of course you can. All it takes is a short little ceremony and voilà—we're husband, wife and baby."

And it really would be just that simple. The only problem was that, in her heart, she'd be forever bound to him. How did she know he'd feel the same? She just couldn't risk it. There was too much at stake. Not just her own emotional well-being, but that of her son. What if she said yes, and then Colby turned out to be less than wonderful after all? What if, like his own father, he got tired of the whole family thing and moved on to greener pastures? Yes, there was no doubt in her mind she could take care of herself and son all on her own, but how would she mend the hole that Colby's leaving would make in their little boy's spirit? On her soul?

"I see that mind of yours working a mile a minute," he said. "Remember our talk about faith?"

She squeezed him for all she was worth.

"That's it. Lean on me. I promise you that, together, we can make this thing work."

I PROMISE WE CAN MAKE this thing work.

Friday afternoon, Whitney was back in her Kodiak Lodge room, gazing across the lake. Cold rain pelted the windows, and the gloom suited her mood.

Rubbing her belly, she crossed the room to ease onto the bed, flipping through channels with the remote.

When Dot and the man she'd been introduced to as Colby's friend Brody had arrived back at the cabin to pick them up bright and early that morning, she'd actually been sad to pack up and let the place go. She'd expected to be angry with her kidnappers, but on the contrary, she was grateful to them for allowing her that wondrous, all-too-brief time with the father of her son.

Still full from a late hearty breakfast of ham and eggs and what had felt like gallons of milk pushed on her by Nugget, Whitney flipped off the TV. Maybe all she needed was a nap. But that didn't work, either, as she missed the wind whispering through towering spruce and Colby's gentle snores.

Their last night at the cabin, he'd shared the big bed with her. That had been the best, having him hold her just as he had that long-ago night on the snowy mountain. Being in his arms again had been a dream she hadn't even known she'd wanted to come true.

Hugging Colby's Santa hat—her guilty souvenir of their first happy night—she grunted as she rolled onto her side, toying for what felt like the gazillionth time since her arrival with the idea of throwing caution to the wind and marrying Colby.

He was warm and funny and handsome and smart.

He was everything she'd ever wanted in a father for her child, and everything she'd never dared hope for in a husband. Back when she'd sat around with her girlfriends giggling late into the night about guys, a man with all his qualities was what she'd claimed to be holding out for. So now that she had him, why couldn't she keep him?

Because there was no such thing as *keeping* a husband, as her mother had all-too-painfully learned. For that matter, even keeping a boyfriend was tough, as Rocco had shown her.

True, but if what she and Colby shared was different? Better? After all, they had the common bond of a child.

Oh—as if her parents hadn't had a child when they'd divorced?

Like Colby's parents hadn't had one when his dad left town?

Scooting up in bed, Whitney tucked Colby's hat under her pillow and switched the TV back on.

She found a repeat of *Trading Spaces,* and reached for her trusty can of squirt cheese on the bedside table. It was empty, as was her bag of licorice.

Arms crossed, legs crossed at the ankles, she'd resigned herself to spending the afternoon rating Frank and Doug's latest designs when a knock sounded at her door.

Startled, she put her hand to her belly, then smoothed her hair into a neat ponytail. "Who is it?"

"Me." Colby.

Hooray! Now there was some entertainment.

As fast as possible with a stomach the size of hers, she crossed the room to open the door, then pulled him into a hug. "I thought you had to fly to Global this afternoon."

"I did. I went fast, so I could get back to you."

"How sweet. Thank you."

"You're welcome," he said, kissing her full on her lips while cradling his hands on either side of the baby. "So? You ready?"

"For what?"

"Your grand tour?"

"Of what?"

He kissed her again. "What do you think? Kodiak Gorge."

"COLBY!" Whitney complained on the tenth dusty stair of Schlump's Hardware. The creaky old staircase was dark and musty—downright spooky. She found it odd that the hardware store was on the town tour, but Colby insisted she had to see the supposedly haunted building.

She sneezed.

"Bless you."

To use him as both protection against ghosts and a tow line, she tucked her fingers into his back pockets. "I'm exhausted. Are we almost there?"

"Just a couple more steps." At the top, he stood aside to make room for her, then said with a flourish of his hands, "Ta-da!"

All she saw was an equally dusty, dank and gloomy hallway, at the end of which creepy pale red light spilled through a stained-glass window. She flinched when something scurried into the room two doors down from where they stood.

"This isn't funny," she said. "People catch diseases from places like this."

"Oh, quit complaining," he said. "Where's your sense of adventure?"

"Back at the lodge. I think I smelled home-baked peanut butter cookies—and you know how much Nugget wants me to drink milk."

As he took her by the hand, Whitney caught him rolling his eyes. "That man's poured enough milk down you to open a dairy."

"Colby!" Reddening, she swatted his behind.

"Is it just me, or have you been doing an awful lot of butt touching on this trip?"

"No!"

"Not that I'm complaining, but..." Leaning against a wall that had been papered in old newspapers, he slipped his hands around her waist, lowering his mouth to hers for a delicious kiss.

"Mmm..." she teased. "This tour is definitely looking up."

"Any idea where you are?" he asked.

"The perfectly dreadful second story of Schlump's Hardware?"

"Nope." He kissed her nose. "You happen to be standing in a piece of Kodiak Gorge history."

"Oh?" She raised her eyebrows, trying not to breathe for fear of contracting some rare form of lung disease from all the dust.

"This very spot happens to be the infamous Dot's Bordello."

Whitney choked on her saliva. "Dot? Our Dot ran a bordello?"

"Nah, her great-grandmother."

"Oh, cool! Dot's grandma was a lady of the night. A shady lady."

"And in this room right here," he said, dragging her into the same room the scurrying thing had vanished into, "Schafer Kingsley shot Barnabas Riley in cold blood for sleeping with Felicity Holmes."

Whitney grimaced, taking a backward step, but Colby pulled her alongside him. Driving rain hit the room's only window.

Whitney shivered.

"The event was in all the papers from Anchorage to San Francisco. Schafer shot the poor bastard straight through his family jewels. That night, Felicity hanged herself off the second-floor balcony."

"What happened to Schafer?"

"He was publicly hanged a week after that."

"And you brought me here why?" Whitney asked, walking deeper into the gloom, the soles of her sneakers cracking broken glass.

"Well, first off, because the place is famous. It's been on two Travel Channel ghost show specials and starred in its very own History Channel documentary on untamed Alaska."

"Oh."

"Still not impressed?"

"Well… It's more than sad, Colby, it's—"

"Tragic," he said, tucking his arms around her. "If you come here at, say, 2 a.m., folks say you can still see Barnabas and Felicity dancing."

Baby Nick kicked, and Whitney jumped slightly.

Colby grinned. "Somebody's enjoying himself."

"That's because he doesn't know any better. What kind of tourist town is this? Don't you have any fudge or ice cream shops?"

"Rough customer, are you?"

"Yes. I paid a lot for this tour."

"What? One measly kiss?"

"I think we're up to two or three now, thank you very much."

"Yeah, well—"

A cold breeze blew through the room, skittering three yellowed newspapers across the wood floor.

"Harvey?" Colby called out, assuming the store's owner must have opened a window. When the chubby proprietor didn't answer, he winked, then said, "Let's get out of here."

"THIS MORE TO YOUR LIKING?" Colby asked a few minutes later, as he led Whitney into the ethereal glow of the town's chapel. The building had been constructed of native stone mined from the gorge, and the pews carved from Sitka spruce. Red carpet, which he'd heard had been a gift to the church from

Dot's great-grandmother, lined the center aisle, and several candles flickered on the altar. Outside, rain still fell, hammering the tin roof.

"It's beautiful," Whitney said.

"The steeple was carted all the way from San Francisco on mules."

"The whole way?"

"Well, not the whole way. I imagine part of the journey was by ferry, but still."

"Do you ever attend services here?"

"Occasionally. I used to come more, when Mom was still in town. She dragged me every Sunday when I was a kid."

"I think it'd be nice being part of a church like this."

Colby caught a wistful edge to Whitney's simple statement. "Your family never went to church?"

"My dad's a philosophy professor. He's also an atheist."

"For real?"

Walking a few steps ahead of him into the hushed place, she nodded.

"Wow. How 'bout your mom?"

"She's never much said one way or the other."

Hence Whitney's problems with the whole faith issue? How could she believe in letting a higher power work things out for the best if she didn't believe in said power at all? "And you?"

"I spent a summer helping out a Peace Corps

friend of mine in Senegal. Pretty standard stuff. We helped build a village clinic. When it was done, people from miles around came to see the doctor. Little kids with strange growths coming out of their backs and heads. Old people blind from cataracts that here in America would be fixed in a routine outpatient procedure.'' Staring straight ahead, she ran her fingers back and forth along the smooth back of a pew. "I saw a man in his prime die from an infected wound on his ankle. I saw a woman die of old age, surrounded by those she loved. I saw three babies born, and those births, more than anything else, made me see what a miracle life is. A crazy, happy miracle none of us have any idea how to control.''

"Yeah, but you can do your dead level best to guide it.''

"You think?''

"Yeah, I do.''

"Okay, so what happened to us on that mountain—who could've predicted that? You yourself checked the weather before we left and said it was safe for flying. We both thought we were going to croak, yet we lived. I never would've dreamed I'd become pregnant practically the first time out of the gate, yet all of it happened.''

"Your point being?''

Shaking her head, she grinned, sliding onto the pew beside him. "I guess that *is* my point—that there's no rhyme or reason to any of what we go through."

"If that's the case, why fight it? Why not just go along for the ride?"

"Because I can't. I have to be in control."

"Why?" He took her hand, rubbed the tender spot between her thumb and forefinger.

"I guess because, growing up, I never once felt secure. Not until I'd entered college and could follow my own set of rules."

"Which included no men, because men hurt you."

"Yes."

He gave her hand a squeeze. "Not all men, Whitney. Not me."

"I know," she said. "That's what makes this decision over whether or not to marry you all the harder. Yes, after the time we've spent together, leaving you would be one of the hardest things I've ever done. But if I marry you, and if we have ten happy years together before our relationship falls apart, that just might be more than I can bear."

Leaning forward, he tried to say *forever* with his gentle kiss. An eternity later, he pulled back, and he whispered, "Marry me, Whitney Foster, and not just for the son I love, but because I love you."

Chapter Fourteen

Whether Whitney believed him or not, Colby meant what he'd said back at the church, and he hoped here, now, in the loft bedroom he'd helped construct with his own hands, he could again use his hands and his heart to build on his relationship with the mother of his son.

"I love you," he said, unzipping the pale blue jacket of her latest jogging suit.

"I love you, too," she said, arching her head back when he kissed her throat. "But I don't know why or even how you could love me. I've given you nothing but grief since I got here."

"True," he teased, easing her jacket off her shoulders and down her arms, letting it fall with a barely audible sound to the carpet. "But every time you annoy me, you have this uncanny knack of reeling me back in." Outside, rain still fell. Inside, he gently drew her white T-shirt over her head, then kissed a trail along the outline of her pretty pink bra. "I loved the way you cared for my cuts after I fell down the lodge stairs."

"I thought you said I was a bad nurse."

"I lied. You were the best. Tender and caring, just the way I'd want you to be with my son." He hooked his thumbs into the waistband of the jogging pants that matched her jacket, tugging them slowly down, letting her use his shoulders for support when he lifted her right foot out, then her left. "I love the way you got so excited over catching a fish, yet you didn't go all squeamish when it came time to eat him—unless I count those tears I saw in your eyes when you thought I wasn't looking. But I will count them, 'cause they tell me you understand Alaska on a basic level—that, up here, nature is a gift to be used but also respected."

"Know what I love about you?" she asked, tugging off his navy-blue T-shirt.

He shivered from the sensation of her cold fingertips on his chest. "You're freezing," he said. "Let's get under the covers."

"I'm fine," she said, planting butterfly-soft kisses along his collarbone and throat. "I love the way every time I turn around, you're wondering if I'm cold. All the time getting me blankets. Tucking in my toes."

"They're cute toes."

"Thanks."

Undoing the top button of his jeans, then another

and another, she knelt before him, kissing each inch of his black cotton boxers that she bared. "I wasn't going to mention this," she said, glancing up at him, eyes sparkling. "But since I'm here, I love how you still wear boxers with stuff on them. These little dancing bears are adorable."

"Yeah, just so long as we keep them a secret just for you."

"Scout's honor," she said, solemnly looking up before bursting into another grin. "Okay, so where was I? Oh—I love the way you didn't yell at me when I let the boat get away."

"That was pretty boneheaded," he teased.

"Oh—and I suppose you could've done better? In case you forgot, right after my knot lesson, you gave me a refresher course on kissing. Could I really be blamed if your second lesson overrode the first?"

"Oh, in that case, I guess you're forgiven."

She gave his jeans an extra hard tug.

"Let's see, I also love your cooking, and the way you forgave me for nearly setting your cabin on fire."

"Nearly?" He choked back a laugh. "Seems to me you were well on your way, darlin'."

"Do you want to hear this?"

"Only if it's truthful."

After tugging his jeans the rest of the way off, she stood. "How's this for truth?"

They'd shared many kisses over the week, even more during their wild night in his plane, but none came close to rocking him the way this one did. It was not only the first time they'd kissed with their true feelings exposed, but the first in broad daylight with her big, bare belly rubbing his.

What a turn-on. He'd done that.

He'd made a baby—well, not entirely on his own, but he had played a big part in his son's creation.

Falling to his knees, he kissed the miracle inside his wife-to-be's stomach. While she clung to his hair, he pulled her pink cotton panties down, helping her step clear. Then he was fumbling at her back to unhook her bra and wishing he was more of a ladies' man when it came to removing lingerie.

"Dammit," he said. "Why the hell don't they make these things with an emergency release?"

She laughed, parking his hands on her full breasts before reaching back to accomplish the task herself. "You know," she said, "I think you actually did a better job of that in the dark in the cramped cargo area of your plane."

"You're right. Probably felt more like the backseat of a parked car."

"Oh, so you were one of those guys, huh?"

He laughed. "I wish. There were four kids in my graduating class—all four of them guys. My friend Brody's girl, Raven, was a junior, but she'd been pretty much taken since the all-school picnic back in sixth grade."

"Bummer."

"My thoughts exactly."

"Well, you big stud—finally, here's your chance to have your way with a naked, willing woman." Grinning, she held out her arms. Laughing right along with her, he tried smoothly getting her into bed, then positioning himself on top of her, but the task proved tougher than he'd planned.

Lying on his side, his hand in the hollow of her hip, he said, "Okay, is it just me, or does Nick make for a logistical nightmare in, um, certain adult areas?"

Bunching pillows under her head, Whitney said, "Seems to me you'll just have to get more creative to reach our goals."

"I will, huh?"

She winked. "After all, you're the one who got me this way."

"Woman, are you always going to be sassy?"

She took a second to think, then said, "Uh-huh."

"Okay, then, guess I'll just have to learn to live with it."

And learn he did.

He started by hushing up that smart mouth of hers, making it impossible for her to speak, only to moan.

"Colby, I—"

"Shh," he said, tucking his head between her knees to have a little fun.

"Ohhh." She braced her fingers in his hair, tugging so hard he winced. He repeated that trick with his tongue—the one that had gotten her hot even in driving snow. Judging by how much harder she was now pulling his hair, he guessed she still liked that particular move.

Whitney squirmed, but the magician between her legs held her in place, nipping her inner thighs, kissing that little—*"Ohhh!"* She wanted him to stop, but at the same time never stop. The sensation was maddening.

He tried shifting on top of her, and she tried making way, wanting nothing more than to let him complete the job he'd started, but there was no getting past her belly.

"Um, let me try something else," he said, shimmying free of his boxers before going for another position. But that didn't work either, and they landed in a tangle of sensation-flooded limbs right back where they'd started.

"What're we going to do?" she asked, by this time feeling more than a little desperate. The things that man did with his tongue!

He sat up and raked his fingers through his hair. "Okay, let's think. We're two reasonably intelligent adults, surely we can—aha."

"What?"

In wickedly sexy, straightforward terms, he spilled his plan in her ear. When she'd thoroughly reddened, he asked, "Think it'll work?"

She showed her approval with another kiss.

EVEN THOUGH HE WAS exhausted from the second wild night he'd shared with Whitney, Colby still couldn't sleep. Around 6:00 a.m., he quit trying in favor of making his future wife a big breakfast.

Funny, but when he'd first gotten home from the cabin, he'd taken a quick shower then headed back out, not wanting to be alone. But now that he had Whitney and his future son with him, the place felt like home again, and he never wanted to leave.

Figuring Whitney would be extra hungry, he whipped up a batch of waffles and link sausage, accompanied by some cantaloupe Henry had left on his doorstep, with a note explaining it had been on sale at the town grocery.

Once he'd assembled two plates on a tray, wishing he had a daisy or something to make it more romantic, Colby grinned. Yep, to be thinking of daisies at this hour made it official.

He had to be in love.

Whistling his way through the sun-flooded house, he took the stairs two at a time, anticipating the view at the top. And he wasn't disappointed to find his very own sleeping beauty still snoring away, gorgeous bare legs tangled in sheets.

Setting the tray on the nightstand on his side of the bed, he slid back under the covers beside her, taking a moment just to drink her in. God, she was beautiful, with her long hair fanning around her pillow and her complexion golden from all their time spent up at the cabin in the sun.

She rolled over, baring her full left breast, and the little boy in him couldn't resist having a little more fun.

An hour later, while Colby was in the kitchen nuking the waffles and sausage, Whitney lounged in his great big whirlpool tub, munching on sweet, cubed cantaloupe.

What an incredible night—and morning—she thought, gazing out the wall of windows overlooking the rugged gorge. The first time she'd seen it, she'd thought it intimidating, but now she saw it as a challenge. Just like she'd conquered her fear of being with this intoxicating man, one day she might conquer Alaska.

One day.

Her latest bite of cantaloupe turned sour in her mouth, making it hard to swallow.

Her heart lurched, and she feared she might be choking.

Oh—she was choking all right.

Not on the fruit Colby had so lovingly prepared, but on her own stupid fears. *One day,* meaning she still wasn't quite ready to commit. *One day,* maybe, but certainly not today. That would be all right. Colby was an understanding guy. She'd go back to Chicago, have their son, and just as soon as he had some free time, he could hop over for a visit.

For that matter, once Nick was big enough to travel, the two of them could come up for visits, and then—

"Here you go."

She lurched, splashing water onto the fluffy red rug in front of the tub.

"Sorry," he said, setting the food tray on the wide red tile ledge. "I didn't mean to sneak up on you."

"I know," she said, swallowing back tears. She didn't want to discuss this. Not now, when everything between them was so right. Her plane left Anchorage that evening, so she still had plenty of time before she'd have to hightail it to the lodge to pack. Until then, she wanted to enjoy the precious hours they had left.

"What's wrong?" he asked, taking his plate, then sitting on the ledge beside her. "You seem upset."

"Let's not talk about it now. I just want to enjoy breakfast. It smells wonderful. Your mom and Nugget did a great job teaching you how to cook."

"Thanks, but back to the subject—what's up?

Are you sick? Did we overdo it last night and... hurt the baby?''

"No, of course not," she said, her hand on his forearm. "I've never felt better."

"Then why the sad eyes?" He set his as-yet untouched plate back on the tray.

"You can probably guess," she said. She looked down. "Think about it. My flight leaves tonight."

"Y-your what?" It was a damned good thing Colby hadn't had a bite of waffle in his mouth, or he'd be dead from sucking it down his windpipe.

Had the woman lost her mind?

Surely he'd misunderstood.

"My flight. I have to get back to Chicago tonight. I still have plans to finalize for the birth and arranging for the nanny to start full-time after my maternity leave. I have bunches more stuff to buy for the nursery. Oh—and I thought I'd pick up one of those— What?"

Jeez, had she just now noticed the anger in his expression?

Smacking his palm against the wall, he said, "Please tell me I didn't just hear you say you're still going to have this baby in Chicago."

"Of course I am. You didn't think I could have it here, did you?"

He hardened his jaw. "If you're worried about not having a doctor, we have a great one. Remember that TV show where the town paid for the doctor's med school if he'd agree to spend a chunk of time practicing there? We did the same thing. Doc Meadows is nice. You'd like her. I'll get you her number and you can make an appointment." On his feet, arms crossed, staring out at the postcard-perfect view, he said. "If you don't want to get married, that's…fine. Just please—don't go."

He looked back to see tears streaming down her cheeks as she awkwardly tried getting out of the tub. She almost slipped, but caught herself. He wanted to be the one catching her, holding her, toweling her dry, but he guessed it was time he realized she could take care of herself.

"Colby…" He held out a thick green towel. Her lips curving in a sad half smile, she took it and wrapped it around herself. "I'm so sorry, but—"

"You're sorry?" He choked on a bitter laugh.

"I can't stay. I can't marry you."

When he turned away from her, clenching his fists, she stretched out one hand and turned him back.

"I'm not saying I might not some day change my mind, I just need more time to study the dynamics of the whole marriage thing. My favorite area of study has been group dynamics under extreme conditions. But I'll for sure take an extra look at marriage. You know, to see just how many of them work. I've looked into dysfunctional relationships, but I'll check into the positive side as well."

"So that's all the thought of marrying me is to you? Just one more case study?"

"Think of the baby, Colby. Do we really want to subject him to us breaking up, if in a couple of years—or maybe even months—from now, we decide our relationship isn't going to work out?"

"Fine, Whitney. I give up." So furious he doubted he could even be civil, Colby started to walk out, but before he left, he had one more thing to say. "I thought last night—hell, this whole week—was magic, but then what do I know, right?" He laughed. "I'm just some country boy you picked up on one of your field studies. As for our son, I'm sure you'll see him as just a convenient little study package, too."

"Colby, I—"

"Don't," he said, the cords in his neck tight. "Don't you dare spout some highbrow academic explanation for your cowardly behavior. And that's just what you are, Whitney Foster, a great big coward too damned afraid to start off on what could've been the best trip of your—no, both of our—lives."

"Please, Colby," she said, crushing his T-shirt in her hands. "Please try to understand. A long-distance relationship won't be so bad. We can work this out over the phone."

Nostrils flared, eyes cold, he said, "The only thing left to work out is our custody agreement. Get dressed, and I'll take you as far as the lodge. After that…I'll see you in court."

THE RIDE FROM COLBY'S once-enchanted home to the lodge had taken an eternity. Packing in front of a grim-faced Nugget had been another eternity. But now that she was finally on board the charter flight she'd arranged to take her to Anchorage, Whitney knew she was doing the right thing.

The mere fact that it'd been so rough saying goodbye to all these people told her staying would've been unhealthy. It couldn't be good to form such immediate attachments—and she had formed attachments to every coot who'd appeared at the lodge to say goodbye.

Henry, still wearing his tired old fedora, hugging her so tight it hurt, tucked a bag of his sweet-smelling pipe tobacco in her pocket—just in case after the baby was born she wanted to take up smoking. Stanley, bringing her a bouquet of forget-me-nots that only served as a reminder of the flower-dotted boulder beside Colby's dock. Nugget, sending her off on her journey with a still-warm plate of foil-wrapped peanut butter cookies and a thermos filled with nice, cold milk.

"You all buckled in back there?" the pilot asked. This was far different from the time she'd flown with Colby. The plane was bigger, and she sat in a seat two behind and to the right of the middle-aged, balding pilot, whose matter-of-fact concern reminded her of carpooling with one of her friends' fathers. Nothing about him was remotely similar to Colby, and as her new pilot rambled through the standard commercial flight safety pitch, Whitney's throat ached from missing the man she loved.

The pilot glanced over his shoulder. "You okay?"

"I'm fine," she said, silent tears streaming down her cheeks as he revved the plane's engine. She'd long since taken Colby's Santa hat from her purse. Gripping it like a lifeline, she was still crying as the plane's floats clacked over Kodiak Lake's choppy water.

You a virgin?

Crying, grinning, peering out over the rapidly fading view, she touched her fingers to the small oval window.

Nope. She was officially no longer even an almost-virgin. But since she knew no man would ever come close to giving her what she'd cherished in Colby, she also knew she'd probably never make love with anyone else.

"Want anything to eat or drink?" the pilot asked over the engine's dull hum. "I've got some pop and pretzels in a cooler behind the back seat."

"No, thank you." *I'm never eating again.*

"Sorry it took me so long to get over here. Had

to repair a busted fuel line. Damnedest thing. We've had a mouse problem back at the hangar. Looks like one of the little buggers must've chewed right through it.''

''That's okay,'' Whitney said, knowing full well nothing would ever be okay again. What had she done?

Oh, she knew from the crushing pain in her chest that she'd made the right decision in leaving. It was coming here in the first place that was now causing her doubts.

Just like her lawyer had said, she should've informed Colby via mail that he was going to be a parent. It would've been clean, efficient. No fuss, no muss.

Oh, so that's what this week was to you, Whitney? Fuss and muss?

Even with a few squabbles, this week had given her a glimpse of familial heaven—a place she'd never even dreamed existed.

Wiping away still more tears, she straightened in her seat.

This was crazy. For the sake of Nick, she had to pull herself together.

Nick. Ugh, even thinking her baby's new name brought on a surge of grief over having to say goodbye.

If leaving was so right, how come it was turning out to be so hard?

Up in front, she noticed a lot of tapping on the controls. Remembering what'd happened after Colby had done the same thing, she asked, "Is everything all right?"

"Yep." He frantically flipped a few more switches before the engine sputtered and died.

Pale pink fluid streamed across Whitney's window.

Fuel?

"Mayday! Mayday!" the pilot shouted into the radio.

Whitney, eyes wild, hugged her belly, bracing her feet.

No, no, no.

This couldn't be happening again!

What were the odds of a person surviving two plane crashes?

Nil.

Absolutely nil.

Ironically, the same odds of ever finding a more perfect husband for herself or a more perfect father for her baby than the very man she was trying to escape.

Oh, dear God, what'd she done? She never should've left. She never should've—

"Hold tight, ma'am! We're going down!"

Chapter Fifteen

"Hey, man, how you doing?"

Colby glanced up from the beer he'd been nursing at the lodge's bar to see his old pal Brody standing there wearing a sympathetic look. "News travels fast round here, huh?"

"What do you mean?"

"Oh, come on," he said. "The news about me being dumped by Whitney. Guess you and I are destined to be bachelors forever, huh?" He raised his long-neck beer. "Let's toast—to bachelorhood."

Brody took the beer, and slid it down the bar. "I'm sorry about your girl, but we just got an emergency call. You sober enough to fly?"

Colby rubbed his eyes, forcing himself instantly alert. "Yeah. I've just had half of this one."

"Cool. Let's rock and roll."

After standing, then leaving a few bills on the bar, Colby asked, "Who's in trouble? Lost hiker?"

On their way out of the bar's gloom and into the lobby's obnoxiously bright light, Brody shook his head. "Downed plane."

"YOU DID A GREAT J-JOB landing," Whitney said, unable to stop her teeth from chattering despite the warm sun and two blankets. Why hadn't she worn a nice practical jogging suit and sneakers instead of this stupid black linen dress, black leather pumps and black panty hose now sporting a run?

"Relax." The pilot, seated beside her on a flat-topped boulder on the lake's shore, patted her back. "We're fine. Help is already on the way. On a clear day like this, shouldn't be but twenty or thirty minutes till we get another ride."

"You're sure?"

"Absolutely," he said, giving her one more fatherly pat.

After the repaired fuel line had apparently broken again, he'd landed the plane smoothly on a small lake that reminded Whitney of the one facing Colby's cabin, only without the snowcapped mountain. Pretty as you please, the plane had drifted to shore, and the pilot had jumped out, towing it the rest of the way in before helping her off. She hadn't even gotten her feet wet.

Then why was she so cold?

Same old song.

Fear.

Only now, it was fear that Colby wouldn't take her back. Although the so-called crash landing had turned out to be no big deal, those moments of wondering whether she'd live or die had seemed more like hours. Through it all, the one topic on her mind was regret. She deeply regretted not handling things differently with the man she now knew she loved.

Yes, she wanted a sweet little wedding attended by all her new friends. Yes—she wanted a three-tiered cake and a forget-me-not bouquet, and a wedding dress hand sewn from Kodiak Lodge T-shirts if only it bound her to Colby forever.

She'd been a fool. Hiding behind fear.

Ironic how it was fear that'd finally shaken her free from her doubts about marriage. On the verge of dying, she finally realized that in loving Colby, she wasn't losing her heart, but gaining her soul.

Faced with death, she'd found faith.

Faith that whether she'd lived or died, she'd loved and been loved. But just the knowing wasn't enough. Now that she was very much alive, she wanted the joy of living.

From the east came the buzz of one plane, then two.

"We're saved!" she said, tossing off her blanket to crush her pilot in a hug.

He cast her a *told you so* look before she awkwardly climbed down from the rock, teetering up and down the shore on her stupid heels, waving her arms.

Wincing from the sun's glare on the broad expanse of water, Whitney put her hands to her forehead, heart pounding at the view. There were two planes—the first she recognized as the one Colby's friend Brody had flown the night of the blizzard. The other belonged to none other than the man she hoped would be her husband within a matter of days—hours if they could find a willing preacher. She didn't need any fancy cakes, dress or flowers. All she needed was him.

As if performing in a precision air show, the approaching pilots landed their planes in tandem before smoothly gliding the rest of the way across the lake. The closer they came, the more she smelled exhaust from their engines mixing with the rich scents of the fishy-smelling water and pungent spruce.

Though her heart was still racing, her spirits soared.

Those scents were Colby's scents, and the first thing she planned to do when she saw him was give him a fiercely apologetic hug.

With the engines off, all fell quiet on the lake, save for the breeze shushing through the trees and small, lapping waves rolling ashore.

Brody stepped out onto his plane's float. ''Some excitement, eh, Vic?'' he shouted to her pilot. Vic.

She'd been so terrified thinking she'd never see Colby again she hadn't even asked the man's name.

Colby's friend Tanner also climbed out of Brody's plane.

"Yep," Vic said. "It was touch and go there for a few minutes, but the old girl did me good."

"I'll say," Brody said, tying his plane to a fallen tree, then crunching along the pebbled shore to help Vic inspect his engine.

He hadn't even looked at *her.*

Hadn't even said *hi.*

What'd you expect? It's probably no big secret that you ran off with his best friend's son!

Chest tight, throat aching from a fresh round of approaching tears, Whitney pressed her hands to her baby, then set off across the shore to Colby's plane.

At the same time, he climbed out.

Sergei followed, but when she approached, he cast her an arctic look before heading over to Vic.

Ignoring him and his cold shoulder, she waddled the rest of the way to Colby, throwing herself into his arms. Tears followed in an uncontrollable gush. "I'm so glad to see you," she said against his chest, loving his strength and smell and sheer breadth. "Yes, I'll marry you," she cried. "I'm so sorry to have been such a fool back at your house this morning. W-when I thought we were going to die—I-it was horrible, Colby."

"I can imagine," he said, awkwardly patting her back instead of murmuring comforting words into her hair. Instead of lifting her up for the reunion kiss she'd spent the past endless minutes dreaming about.

"Colby?" She slowly unclasped her fingers from where she'd clenched his T-shirt, which was still damp from her tears.

"I'm thrilled that you and the baby are safe," he said, "but…"

"But what? Didn't you hear me? You don't have to be mad at me anymore. I've seen the light—literally," she added on the heels of a nervous laugh. "You were right—about everything. Oh, Colby, we'll make a beautiful family, and I do trust you, and love you, and our life is going to be just great."

A muscle ticked in his hardened jaw, and instead of their usual warm sea-green, his eyes had grown stone cold.

"Now that we know you're okay," he said, "Brody's gonna ferry you and Vic back to Anchorage so Vic can grab some parts, and you don't miss your flight."

Her heart thundering as though an entire sled dog team was racing through her chest, Whitney gave another nervous laugh. "Yeah, but didn't you hear? I'm not going to Anchorage. To heck with catching my flight." She threw herself at him in another hug, but just when she'd gotten comfortable, he gripped her shoulders, lightly pushing her away.

"Yes, Whitney. You're leaving. Now." He whistled and Brody looked in their direction. "Vic, whenever you're ready, Brode's gonna ferry you back to get a new line."

Vic nodded, then knelt to gather the few tools he'd already spread on the ground.

"Colby?" Whitney began to tremble all over. "Colby, please. Didn't you hear me? I want to marry you. I love you. Look—I even have proof." More than a hint of desperation in her tone, she ran as best she could the short distance to her purse to get Colby's hat. "Look," she said, waving it on her short trip back to his side. "I know I shouldn't have, but I took this the night we were rescued. I was wrong, Colby—about everything. I loved you then, only I was too afraid to admit having fallen for you in only one, incredible night."

"My hat? That's your so-called proof?" He laughed. "While I'm flattered I was a good enough date that you wanted a souvenir, some corny Santa hat doesn't mean you love me, Whit. You could've died. You were understandably scared. But scared doesn't equal love—not after that proper little speech you delivered just a few hours ago back at the house. In fact, I'll bet if you think hard enough, you could even come up with a label to identify your sudden change of feelings. Maybe some kind of Stockholm Syndrome thing.''

''How can you say that? You don't know what's going on in my heart!''

Toying with the tether rope to his plane, he said, ''Better than anyone, Whitney, I do know what's going on inside you, and it ain't pretty. Emotionally, you're a scared ten-year-old living in a grown woman's body. You have this academic view of the world, neatly assembling every emotion and person into textbook-perfect case studies—but you know what? I don't want to fit into one of your studies. I want to be the *only* study. I wanted to be your whole life, just like I offered to be yours. But you turned me down one too many times and now I rescind the offer.'' Stepping onto the float, in front of Sergei and Tanner, he said, ''Somehow, we'll reach an equitable custody agreement, but as for the two of us being a couple—we're history.''

''Yo, Whitney!'' Brody shouted. ''Your ride's back here!''

One trembling hand on her baby, she put her other over her mouth, not caring who saw her tears.

How could he do this me? How could he be so cruel?

Stupid questions considering how often she'd been cruel to him. Belittling his desire to raise his son. Not trusting him to be a kind and caring husband to her. Yet again, he'd been right in his biting words, only now there was nothing she could do to repair the damage she'd done.

She lowered her hand from her mouth to try apologizing once more, but it was too late. By the time she figured out what to say, he was already back in his plane, waving at her to step back.

When she refused to budge, to break her stare, Brody slipped his arm loosely about her shoulders, guiding her to his plane. "I'm real sorry," he said. "You two would've made a good team."

"Then talk to him, Brody. *Please.* Make him understand that—"

"Shh…" Brody squeezed her shoulders. "It's over," he said while Colby started his plane's engine. "You gotta face facts. It's over."

"But I love him!"

"Really?" he asked, even as Colby backed his plane away.

"I think I do." Swallowing hard, she added, "Isn't that enough?"

Brody laughed sadly, guiding her the rest of the way toward his plane. "For Colby, nope. *Thinking* isn't anywhere near enough. He's your basic all-or-nothing kind of guy."

THAT NIGHT AT THE LODGE BAR, Colby stared at the tall-neck beer in front of him. It'd been staring back at him for going on nearly an hour now, but he still hadn't taken a drink.

Some drunken fool had put about twenty bucks' worth of my-wife-left-me-and-took-my-'57 Chevy-with-her country music on the jukebox, and Colby's head throbbed in time with the blinking neon Coors sign behind the bar.

Brody should've been back by now.

What an afternoon—hell, he might as well go a little further and include the whole damn week.

The way that woman played him ought to be criminal.

She'd played with his heart like a dog with a rawhide chew toy. And then saying some goofy hat proved she'd changed her mind and loved him. That was crazy. Just plain nuts. People didn't change all of a sudden. They just didn't. And if anyone should know that, it was Whitney. After all, she was the one with all those damned book smarts.

"How you doin'?" Tanner asked, easing onto the stool beside him.

"How do you think?"

"You ever gonna drink that beer?" he asked. "Polnick says that's the last one, then we're gonna have to switch to tap 'til he gets another shipment."

Polnick was the bartender currently shoveling his way through a plate of Nugget's lasagna.

"Take it," Colby said. "Guess I'm not in the mood for drinkin'."

"Wanna fly down to Cordova, then? See if we can score?"

"Jeez, Tanner." Colby scowled. "Way to go on the sensitivity there, bud. No wonder Jenny left you."

"What? Because she left, I'm supposed to be a hermit?"

"You made a lifelong vow to be faithful to her, remember?"

After taking a long swig of his newly acquired beer, he said, "She's the one who left me. I'd say that pretty much cancels any and all agreements."

Colby shook his head. "I'm outta here. Catch ya later."

Tanner grabbed Colby's sweatshirt sleeve, yanking him back. "You know what your problem is, Davis?"

"Why don't you tell me, McCormick." Colby steeled his jaw. Closed his hands into fists.

"You're just too damned loyal. Like a big old hound dog, just waitin' around for a pat on your dumb, blind head."

"You're wasted," Colby said through gritted teeth, "so I'm gonna pretend you didn't say that."

As if sensing a fight, the guys in back stopped playing pool to watch.

"Pretend all you want, bud, but that girl played you like a fiddle. Hell, she's probably back in Chicago right now, chatting up some guy she met in the airport lounge. Hell, how do you even know that baby she's carrying is yours? What if she's not even pregnant? Like she's just messin' with your mind? Like some UFO conspiracy thing, that—''

Smack.

Colby hit his so-called friend hard and fast, right across the jaw.

In slow motion, Tanner fell off the stool, cracking the back of his head on the bar.

Colby was ready to give him another blow at the first smartass comment out of his mouth, but a bunch of guys stepped in to stop him.

"Let him be," somebody said.

"He's just drunk. He didn't mean anything."

"You'll be all right." Someone patted him on his back.

No. No, Colby knew he wasn't anywhere near all right, and he feared he might never be again. Jeez, he'd just hauled off and slugged one of his best friends.

Colby held out his hand to Tanner to help him up, but Tanner batted it away.

"I was just tellin' you the truth," Tanner said, spitting blood on Colby's right hiking boot.

"Yeah, well, next time, keep it to yourself."

"Come on, there, big fella," Polnick said to Tanner, helping him to his feet.

Tanner wobbled for a second before regaining his footing, then took one look at Colby and swung.

The fight was back on.

"WELL, KID," Brody said, standing at the security gate for Whitney's flight. "Guess this is it."

The strength of her sudden hug in the midst of a human river of traffic moved him to the point that after she let go, it took him a few seconds to regain his composure.

After dropping off Vic, she'd had three hours to kill before her flight, so he'd taken her to a hole-in-the-wall beer joint that served good burgers and even better onion rings. They'd talked for every minute of those hours, and she'd told him the whole story, right down to the secret she'd only just told Colby—she'd fallen hard for him that first night they were together, but was too afraid of losing him to ever claim him in the first place. She'd also told Brody that in the back of her mind she wondered if she hadn't returned to Kodiak Gorge to do exactly that—claim her man. Her baby's father.

Standing here now, watching her blink back tears, Brody knew his heart couldn't take it a minute longer.

He'd known Colby literally all his life, so he figured if anyone had a right to interfere in that life, he was the one.

Grasping Whitney's small, cold hands, he asked, "You like surprises?"

The hope lighting her face transformed her from a sad little girl to a full-on gorgeous woman. Brody's chest tightened. If she weren't already carrying his best friend's baby, he'd have made a play for her himself.

She nodded.

"Then come on. We've got a lot of work to do."

Chapter Sixteen

"Thank you," Whitney said to Brody around midnight when he stopped his truck in front of Colby's house. "For everything."

She slid across the seat to throw her arms around him in a warm hug.

"It was my pleasure." Pulling away, he laughed. "I just wish I could be around to see the look on Colby's face when you show up at his door."

Whitney nibbled on her lower lip. "Do you think he'll take me back?"

"Remember, you're in Alaska now. Time for you to assert yourself. This isn't a matter of giving the man a choice, Whitney, it's telling him how it's going to be."

"You're right. I'm in control." She fumbled with the door's handle, then felt her old familiar fears return. "Funny," she said, finally shoving the door open. "If I'm in control, how come I feel faint?"

Laughing again, he climbed out to carry her bags to the porch, then they walked back to his truck.

"You'll be fine," he said, climbing behind the wheel. "Now get out of here so I can go home and get some shut-eye."

With one last hug, Brody was gone, save for the faint smell of exhaust hanging in the air, and the glow of his taillights through the dirt road's dust.

Well, this is it, Whitney thought, straightening her shoulders for the march up to the house that— if all went well—would soon be her home. Either Colby would take her back, or she'd spend the next couple of days out here sleeping with the bears, because one thing was for sure. She wasn't leaving until Colby hadn't just given her an answer, but the *right* one!

Her footsteps sounded abnormally loud on the porch steps when the only sounds they had to compete with were the whining bugs. In the airport rest room, she'd changed out of her black dress and heels into a comfy pair of maternity jeans and a pink sweatshirt. She'd never realized sneakers could clomp so loudly.

Her stomach growled.

Even that was noisy!

Heart pounding, mouth dry, she knocked at Colby's door.

There were no lights on inside, just a faint blue glow. She guessed the TV was on in the loft. She knocked again, and when there was still no sign of life, she tried the door, only to find it open.

Terrified, excited, ready to burst into tears at the first sight of the man she loved, Whitney eased the door open and stepped inside before closing it silently behind her.

Her tennis shoes were, thankfully, quiet on the hardwood floor.

From upstairs spilled the laugh track and bouncy music of an old *Seinfeld* episode.

Taking the stairs slowly, she forced herself to breathe, praying Colby was awake since she didn't have the heart to wake him. But she doubted her nerves could stand not knowing his reaction to her return until morning.

At the top of the stairs, she released a deep sigh before approaching the bed. "Colby?" she asked softly.

She crept closer, closer—except that he wasn't there.

On TV, *Seinfeld* faded into a cat-food commercial.

Meow, meow, meow...

If he wasn't in bed, where could he be? She checked in the master bath, but found that empty, too. She deliberately avoided looking at the tub where she'd made the worst decision of her life.

Creeping back downstairs, she glanced at the

couches, thinking he might've fallen asleep there, but nope.

He wasn't in the kitchen, either.

Her stomach growled again, and on her way past the pantry—the pantry that, if all went well, would soon be hers—she opened the door, flipped on the light, then foraged for a can of squirt cheese and a box of her favorite crackers. There they were. Yum. One mission accomplished.

She flicked off the light and was backing out the door, arms loaded with snacks, when from out of the darkness a familiar male voice said, "Stop right there, and put down whatever the hell you're stealing 'cause I'm in no mood to deal with a thief."

"Colby, it's me."

He flicked on the kitchen light, blinking at the sudden glare. "Whitney?" He set a baseball bat on the counter, his shoulders sagging. "What the hell are you doing? I might've hurt you."

"What does it look like I'm doing? I'm fixing a snack."

He shook his head as if to clear it. "Okay, let's back up. Why are you fixing a snack in my house? I thought you'd be in Chicago by now."

Calmly putting her treasures on the counter beside the bat, she flipped open the cracker box, taking a whiff of salty, tangy, spicy goodness. "Mmm...I've been craving one of these all day."

Stepping to the counter to pop the lid on the

cheese, then squirt out a circle atop her cracker, he said, "What're you doing here, Whitney?"

He handed it to her, and she popped the whole thing in her mouth, closing her eyes while she chewed. "Mmm...this is so good."

He rolled his eyes—one of which she now noticed was black. The left side of his jaw was swollen.

She gasped, touching her hand to his bruised cheek. "What happened?"

He flinched from her touch, pushing down her hand. "Nothing. It's no big deal."

"Yes, it is. You've been in a fight."

He shrugged.

"Colby? What happened?" She reached out again to touch him, but again he flinched away.

Oh, boy. She took a deep breath.

Looked like this was going to be tougher than she'd figured. Maybe she should just save all her questions about his fight for another time, and proceed to the next item on her agenda.

Digging into her pocket, she said, "Brody and I had a nice day. He took me out for the best cheeseburger I've ever had, and then we went shopping."

"You and Brody?" Colby nearly choked. First Tanner had been trashing her, and now his friend Brody had been making moves on her? What was this world coming to when not a single one of his friends could be trusted?

"Uh-huh. We went ring-shopping because, just as you've pointed out so many times, this baby of ours is going to need a father."

"Oh. Let me get this straight. Since I turned you down, you went running to Brody and he snapped you up?" Colby didn't think he could feel any more furious than he'd been at the bar, but this...

Snatching up the baseball bat, he stormed to the front door. When he got his hands on that so-called best friend of his, he was going to—

"Colby, wait!" Whitney ran after him, catching him at the door by clutching the back of his shirt. "You misunderstood. It wasn't like that."

Jaw clenched, fingers gripping the bat, he spun around. "Tell me what it was like then. I'd really like to know."

Never had Whitney seen him so enraged—not even the time she'd pulled out those custody papers she'd had her lawyer draw up. Could the fact that he was so insanely jealous at the mere thought of her hooking up with Brody be a sign in her favor? That he still felt *something* for her?

She licked her lips, unsure where to begin.

"I'm waiting," he said, right hand on the door.

His left hand held the bat, so she worked it loose, leaning it against the corner. His hand free, she grasped it, fumbling with his ring, but eventually slipping it on. "Brody took me shopping for your ring—and mine," she said, holding up a matching band. "We can have a proper ceremony tomorrow, but tonight, I want us to have one all our own. I want—"

For the longest time he stood there staring at her, his gaze searching her face for any indication that what she'd said might be another one of her games. But then he must've recognized that she was tired of playing games. All she wanted now was for the two of them to be together—forever.

Colby crushed her in a hug, burying his face in her hair. "I was so scared," he said. "When Vic's plane went down, I kicked myself for not forcing you to stay—for not locking both of us in my pantry and throwing away the key."

"I like it in there," she said with a teary, sniffy giggle.

"I know." He felt shaky. Weak. Rage fell away, making room for the shimmering waves of love he felt for this woman and his child.

"When we came to get you and Vic," he said, "I wanted to take you back right then and there, but my so-called friends told me to let you go. Tanner—he's still so bitter about Jenny leaving him. He told me to forget we'd even met, but I couldn't. I love you."

"I love you, too," she said when he lifted her up for the kiss she'd rehearsed a thousand times in her head. She wrapped her legs around his waist.

He crushed his mouth to hers, almost afraid to

believe she was really there. "I'm sorry I left," she said, her breath hot and moist in his ear.

"No," he said, his fingers buried in her soft hair. "I'm sorry I pushed you. Jeez, of course, you'd have qualms about marrying some guy you've only known a week."

She kissed him again. "I feel like I've known you forever. I think that was the scariest part. Everything we've shared—it's so different from what I thought love should be."

Between them, he felt his son kick, and he set Whitney down. "I didn't hurt the little guy, did I?"

"No," she said with that tinkling laugh he loved. "I think he's just saying hello."

Colby knelt to kiss her belly. "You're gonna have a great life," he said to his son. "We're gonna fish and hike and I'll teach you how to fly."

"What about me?" Whitney asked, her fingers in his hair. "Don't I get to do any of that fun stuff?"

"Fishing and hiking—yes. As for the flying... Woman, I'm never letting you near a plane again."

Epilogue

"Colby, good grief, would you leave the tree alone, and come sit with us by the fire?"

"I want everything perfect."

"It is. Your mom and stepdad and the whole crazy crew is going to love what you've done."

"It's not their opinion I'm worried about," he said, scooping his pride and joy from his momma's arms. "Nick, here's, got to learn how Christmas is done. After all," he added, removing his bedraggled Santa hat to settle it on his son's small head, "conceived like he was on Christmas Eve, he's a real live, Santa Baby."

"Hey," Whitney teased, standing beside him. "I thought I was your Santa Baby?"

He kissed the top of her head. "Can't a guy have two?"

"What are we going to do when we have a daughter one of these days? Maybe another son?"

Their gurgling three-month-old between them,

Colby pulled her into a hug. "Then I guess we'll have a house full of Santa babies. But hey, I thought you wanted a few more years to get your consulting business off the ground before we try for any more?"

"I do, I'm just saying that when the time comes, you'd better watch out."

"…Better not pout?"

Wagging her finger at him, she grinned. "You'd better not cry I'm tellin' you why…"

"Santa Claus is comin'…to town."

They were still laughing and singing carols an hour later when the doorbell rang, and in spilled Colby's family and Vic, who'd flown them in for the occasion.

Whitney's mother and stepfather were coming for a nice, long visit over New Year's. Whitney was looking forward to many fireside chats with her mom, during which, hopefully they could once again learn to be close.

After a buffet meal of ham and turkey and all the trimmings, Colby's step nieces and nephews took baby Nick into the TV room for movies.

Whitney excused herself from the boisterous crowd laughing and sharing stories in front of the fire to make a fresh batch of eggnog.

She jumped when Colby stepped up behind her, but then he eased her into his arms as he placed a string of kisses around her neck, kisses that followed the form of the gold necklace he'd given her the day Nick was born. It had a beautiful gold-and-diamond snowflake charm. "Mmm...I love you," he said.

She turned to face him. "I love you, too."

"It's snowing again."

"And…"

"So, I know the white stuff's been lucky for us, but I'm wondering if next year you want to go somewhere warm for Christmas? Hawaii?"

"Nope. I like it right here in Kodiak Gorge—snow and all." She fingered her charm.

"Yeah, but I was thinking…" He gave her another kiss.

"About what?"

"Well…since I'm in charge of decorations, and Nick and I are sharing the family Santa hat, and since he's now our official Santa Baby—I don't want you feeling left out."

"I don't. I was just teasing about—"

He silenced her with another kiss. "I figured as much, but still…" He released her to dig in his back pocket. "Just so there's no family squabble, I bought you this—only it might be a little cold here for you to truly enjoy it, which is why next year Hawaii might be a better place to spend the holidays."

Whitney raised her eyebrows.

The only thing in her husband's hand was a scrap of red satiny fabric with a teeny bit of green attached. "Um, thanks," she said, "but what is it?"

He beamed. "A Santa baby bikini."

HARLEQUIN®

AMERICAN *Romance*®

A COWBOY AND A KISS

by Dianne Castell

Sunny Kelly wants to save the old saloon
that her aunt left her in a small Texas town.

But Sunny isn't really Sunny.
She's Sophie Addison, a Reno attorney,
and she's got amnesia.

That's not about to stop cowboy
Gray McBride, who's running hard for
mayor on a promise to clean up the town—
until he runs into some mighty strong
feelings for the gorgeous blonde.

On sale starting December 2004—
wherever Harlequin books are sold.

If you enjoyed what you just read,
then we've got an offer you can't resist!

Take 2 bestselling love stories FREE!
Plus get a FREE surprise gift!